THE FIGHTING MAN

Young Rob Sinclair, a homesteader's son in the Wyoming Territory, has never handled a gun. But when the Nolan gang kills his parents, he's determined to bring the culprits to justice. Against the prevailing knowledge that only a real fighting man could defeat the Nolan gang, Rob learns to fight and sets out to search for the killers. He eventually reaches the Texas Panhandle, little knowing what awaits him there. Can he complete such a perilous mission alone?

ALAN IRWIN

THE FIGHTING MAN

Complete and Unabridged

LINFORD
Leicester

First published in Great Britain in 2010 by
Robert Hale Limited, London

First Linford Edition
published 2012
by arrangement with
Robert Hale Limited, London

British Library CIP Data

Irwin, Alan, *1916 –*
    The fighting man.- -
    (Linford western library)
    1. Murder- -Wyoming- -Fiction. 2. Parents- -
    Crimes against- -Fiction. 3. Revenge- -Fiction.
    4. Bounty hunters- -Fiction. 5. Western stories.
    6. Large type books.
    I. Title II. Series
    823.9′14–dc23

    ISBN 978–1–4448–0950–3

Published by
F. A. Thorpe (Publishing)
Anstey, Leicestershire

Set by Words & Graphics Ltd.
Anstey, Leicestershire
Printed and bound in Great Britain by
T. J. International Ltd., Padstow, Cornwall

This book is printed on acid-free paper

1

It was exactly half past one on a sunny afternoon when the robbers raided the bank in the small town of Winslow in Wyoming Territory. One of them remained outside, by the horses. Another stayed just inside the door to intercept any customers who might enter the bank while the robbery was in progress. A third member of the Nolan gang herded into a corner the two customers already in the bank together with the teller and held a gun on them. At the same time Pete Nolan, the leader of the gang, went behind the counter with a six-gun in his hand and walked up to Carter, the manager, who was seated at a desk not far from the counter. There was a revolver in the drawer of the desk but Carter judged that any move towards it on his part would be suicidal.

Nolan was a man of average height

and build. His face was swarthy, ruthless and unshaven. He had a widespread reputation as the leader of a gang of criminals who had no scruples about killing any citizen or law officer who might interfere with their criminal activities. He stopped in front of the manager and glanced at the large metal safe standing on the floor behind him. The door was closed.

'That's a nice big safe you've got there,' said Nolan. 'Let's see what's inside it, shall we? Open it up pronto, or the teller over there will get a knife in the back.' He pointed to the corner where the teller and the two customers stood facing the wall.

The banker groaned inwardly. From his point of view, the robbery could hardly have taken place at a less opportune time. The safe contained a large quantity of banknotes, most of which were due to be collected by Wells Fargo the following day for delivery to a destination to the west. But he could see no alternative but to comply with

Nolan's demand. He rose to his feet, took a key from his pocket, unlocked the door of the safe, and pulled it open.

Nolan's eyes gleamed as he saw the neatly stacked bundles of banknotes inside the safe. Keeping Carter covered, he looked through the drawers of the desk and found the revolver, which he tucked under his belt. He ordered the banker to sit on his chair by the desk.

'Sit there quiet till we're gone,' he said, 'or the teller dies.'

Keeping one eye on the manager, Nolan picked up a canvas sack lying on the bottom of the safe, and quickly stuffed the banknotes into it. Then, well satisfied with his haul, he hurried with it to the door and called to the man guarding the teller and the two customers to follow him. Then he opened the door, and all three ran to the waiting horses, closing the door behind them.

Inside the bank, the manager, as he saw the door close, was galvanized into action. He rushed to the counter and from a concealed pigeonhole underneath it he pulled out a loaded Colt .45 revolver. He ran to the door and cautiously opened it a few inches. Nolan and the others were riding off fast along the street, with Nolan in the lead. Carter fired one shot, directed at the rearmost of the four riders. The rider's mount reared up, but was quickly brought under control. The manager's next shot was well wide of the mark, and before he could fire again, the outlaws had disappeared between two buildings on one side of the street. A few moments later they were clear of town and riding rapidly towards the south.

★ ★ ★

Six miles south of Winslow, homesteader Dan Sinclair had just walked out of his barn when he saw four riders approaching. Two of them were seated on one horse. Another horse was bearing a rider and a spare saddle and bridle. He stood waiting until they rode up to him and stopped. He felt a deep sense of unease as he looked at the four strangers.

'Howdy,' said Nolan. 'We just had a stroke of bad luck. A few miles back there one of our horses stepped in a hole and busted its leg.' He looked over to a small fenced-in pasture close by where a single horse was grazing. The animal was a handsome chestnut, used by the homesteader for occasions when he was riding alone into town or to visit neighbours.

'That's a mighty good looking chestnut over there,' Nolan went on. 'That'll suit us fine. Just name your price.'

'Sorry,' said Dan. 'The chestnut's not for sale. I can't help you. It ain't far to Winslow. The liveryman there will fix you up.'

Nolan's face hardened. 'You just made a big mistake, mister,' he said, pulling out his six-gun, a move which was copied by the three men with him.

Keeping Dan covered, the four men dismounted, and surrounded the homesteader. Turner, the man standing directly behind him, at a nod from Nolan, struck him hard across the head with the barrel of his six-gun. Dan staggered forward a few paces, then collapsed against a stout timber water trough. As he fell, his head collided with the top of one side of the trough. He lay motionless on the ground. Nolan looked down at the unconscious man, then told Turner to see if there was anyone in the house.

★　★　★

Inside the house, nursing a severe cold, Martha Sinclair got up from the bed where she had been taking a brief rest, and went into the living room. She walked to the window to see if there was any sign of her husband outside. She arrived there in time to see him struck savagely on the head by one of four strangers, and collapse behind the water trough, out of her view.

Aghast, she hesitated only for a moment, then ran to take down a double-barrelled shotgun which was hanging on the wall. Then, desperately, she looked through the drawers of a chest for cartridges, and took out two. With trembling fingers she loaded the shotgun and pulled back the two hammers. Holding the gun in front of her, she went back to the partly open front window, failing to see Turner as he looked into the living room through a window in the side of the house.

Looking out, she could see that Dan was still out of sight behind the water trough, and that three of the strangers were standing together at a point not far from the house. She pointed the shotgun at the three men and felt for the trigger. But just before she was able to pull it, a bullet from Turner's six-gun struck her in the back, and she lost her hold on the weapon. As the shotgun hit the floor one hammer sprang forward and a load of buckshot was discharged into the wall of the house. Martha collapsed on the floor.

Startled by the gunfire, Nolan and the two men standing by him watched as Turner ran round to the door and went inside the house. He came out shortly after to tell them what had happened.

'You three were plumb lucky,' he said. 'I shot the woman just in time. She was aiming a shotgun at the three of you. And we all know what damage a shotgun blast can do at that range. I took a look at her. I was right on target. She ain't moving. I figure she's dead.'

Nolan walked over to take a look at Dan. He knelt by him briefly, then stood up and walked back to the others.

'The man's dead as well,' he said. 'I reckon the second knock on the head finished him off. We need to be moving on.'

He told Turner to get the chestnut from the pasture and saddle it, while he and the other two, Haley and Radford, ransacked the house in search of cash. It was Nolan who found the banknotes, to the value of over six hundred dollars, in a tin box at the back of a drawer in a chest in a bedroom. This was the total amount saved by the homesteaders over several years of unrelenting toil. The outlaws left the house with the money, joined Turner outside, and rode off, leaving the bodies of their victims lying where they had fallen. They were heading in a southerly direction, at a fast pace.

★ ★ ★

An hour after Nolan and his men left the homestead, a buckboard approached it from the east. The driver was Rob Sinclair, the twenty-year-old son of Dan and Martha. Rob was tall and well built, with a strong clean-cut face which strongly resembled that of his father. Seated beside him was his eighteen-year-old sister Elizabeth, an attractive young woman, and the apple of her father's eye.

Driving the buckboard past the water

trough, Rob pulled up suddenly as he spotted his father lying on the ground. He jumped down and ran over to kneel beside the body. He saw the two ugly wounds on the head and called out to his father. But there was no response, and no sign of breathing. He was sure that his father was dead.

Standing beside him, Elizabeth looked down with fear and dismay at the motionless body of her father, Sick at heart, Rob's immediate concern was for the welfare of his mother. Taking Elizabeth with him he ran over to the house and went inside. Immediately, they saw their mother lying on her side on the floor under the window. Kneeling beside her, Rob saw the bullet hole in the back of her dress. He called out to her but there was no response. Standing by him, Elizabeth started to cry.

Rob turned his mother to lie on her back, and leaned over to check whether she was still breathing. As he did so, her eyes slowly opened and focused on his face, then that of her daughter.

Elizabeth, sobbing, knelt down beside her mother. Weakly, Martha raised her hands, one towards her daughter, one towards her son. Each of them took hold of a hand, and Rob, seeing that Martha was trying to speak, leaned over her. Her voice was faint, and she paused between the words.

'I saw them knock your father down,' she said. 'Near the water trough. Did you find him?'

Rob nodded. 'He's still lying there,' he said. 'I can't wake him.'

Martha's face twisted with grief. She closed her eyes briefly before speaking again. Her voice now was almost inaudible.

'There were four of them,' she whispered. 'I . . . ' Her voice trailed off, and her head slumped sideways as she stopped breathing. Rob and Elizabeth felt her hands go limp. After a short while they both rose.

'We've got to let them know in town about this,' said Rob, after comforting his sister. They were both trying to come to terms with the sudden loss of two loving parents.

Rob dragged his father's body into the house, and laid him by his wife. Leaving the house, he found that his father's saddle-horse was missing. He and his sister climbed on to the buckboard and headed for town. Halfway there they came on a dead horse lying on the ground. It had been shot through the head. This, thought Rob, could account for the horse missing from the homestead.

When they arrived in town, they stopped outside the livery stable. Rob knew that Hunter, the liveryman, doubled as the town undertaker. Shocked, Hunter listened as Rob told him what had happened at the home-stead.

'I'll tend to your folks,' said Hunter. 'I'll take a buckboard out and bring them back here. But first, we'd better tell Mr Carter at the bank. It looks like the four men who robbed the bank here might be the ones who killed your mother and father. Wait here.'

He went over to the bank, and shortly after returned with the manager. Rob repeated what he had told the liveryman.

'It all fits,' said Carter. 'I'm sure that I accidentally shot one of their horses as they were riding out of town. I was aiming at the rider, but I don't claim to be an expert with a six-gun. I've sent a message to the law in Cheyenne about the robbery. Likely they'll send somebody here to investigate. I'll send another message about your mother and father.'

The banker left, and Rob and his sister waited while Hunter got his buckboard hitched up. Then he accompanied them to the homestead. When the liveryman had departed with the bodies, Rob spoke to his sister. He had known of the cash sum which his parents had painstakingly saved over the years, and he had discovered that it was missing, presumably taken by the killers.

'I've been thinking about what we should do, Elizabeth,' he said. 'I don't want to live here after what's happened to Mother and Father. What I want to do is make sure that the men who did that to them are captured and made to pay for what they did. I don't care how long it takes. So before I start out on that I'm going to take you to Mother's sister in Cheyenne. She'll look after you while I'm gone. You like your Aunt Sarah, don't you?'

Elizabeth, who had spent some time with her Aunt Sarah in the past, nodded her head. She was close to tears, still badly shocked by their loss.

'All right, then,' said Rob. 'I'll take you there as soon as we can get away from here.'

Just after dark, a buckboard drove up to the house. The driver climbed down and knocked on the door. He was a homesteader called Nelson who owned an adjoining quarter section. He was married, with one eighteen-year-old son. Rob opened the door and invited him inside. The two families were good friends and neighbours.

'I don't hardly know what to say, Rob,' said Nelson. 'I was real shocked when I heard the news in town about Dan and Martha. I'm here to see if there's anything we can do to help you both.'

Rob thanked him, then told him of his own decision to ensure that the gang was caught, and of his intention to take Elizabeth to stay with her aunt in Cheyenne while he was so engaged.

'That's a mighty dangerous job you're taking on,' said Nelson. 'Why not let the law handle it?'

'The law's spread mighty thin around here,' said Rob. 'I figured it could do with a helping hand.'

'What about the homestead?' asked Nelson.

'We don't figure on keeping it, after what happened,' said Rob. 'Father worked it long enough to make him the legal owner. We'll try to sell it.'

'I'm sorry to hear that,' said Nelson,

'but there's a chance I can help you there. Like I told your father a while back, I have a brother who used to farm in Illinois. But now he's on his way out here. Should be turning up any time. He's aiming to claim a quarter section in this area. He's not short of money. Got a good price for his farm. I reckon he'll jump at the chance of buying a quarter section, complete with buildings, that's already been licked into shape. Have you got a price in mind, Rob?'

'Not right now,' Rob replied. 'I'll take some advice from Mr Carter at the bank, and let you know.'

2

The following morning Rob and his sister went into Winslow on the buckboard to attend the funeral of their parents, who were buried in the cemetery on the edge of town. The ceremony was well attended. When it was over, Rob and Elizabeth walked with Carter to the bank. There Rob told him of his decision to sell the homestead and take Elizabeth to Cheyenne before embarking on a search for the killers of his parents. He asked the bank manager if he would deal with the legal aspects of the selling of the homestead, mentioning that Nelson's brother was a possible buyer.

'I can do that for you,' said Carter, 'and I can make you a loan, to be paid back when the homestead is sold. But I reckon you should think twice before tangling with those four killers. I got word that a US marshal from Cheyenne will be arriving here soon to check up on the robbery and the killing of your parents. He'll be wanting to talk with you.'

US Marshal Winter arrived in Winslow the following day and, after talking with Carter, he rode out to the Sinclair homestead to hear first hand from Rob about the tragic events at the homestead after the robbery. He listened with interest to Rob's account, and took a description of the stolen horse. He said that from the banker's detailed description of the man who had forced him to open the safe, he was certain that this man was Nolan, the leader of a gang of four outlaws, who specialised in bank and stagecoach robberies, and who had operated in Texas and Colorado as well as in Wyoming.

'I'm mighty sorry about your folks,' said Winter, a tough, square-jawed man in his early fifties with many years as a respected law officer behind him. 'We've never been able to get our hands on the Nolan gang. They're a slippery bunch. Vanish without a trace after each robbery. Maybe we'll be lucky this time. Mr Carter tells me you're taking your sister to kinfolk in Cheyenne, after which you aim to go after the Nolan gang.'

'That's right,' said Rob. 'I just can't rest easy knowing that the killers of my parents are on the loose. So if the law don't catch them for this, I aim to take a hand.'

'The four men in the Nolan gang are all experts with a six-gun and a rifle,' said the marshal. 'I expect you're pretty handy with those weapons yourself?'

'Never had reason to handle them,' said Rob. 'Mother wouldn't have anything like that around. Father had a shotgun that I weren't allowed to touch. But I aim to get me a six-gun and a rifle and get in some practice.'

Looking at the set of Rob's jaw, Winter abandoned the idea of trying to get the speaker to change his mind. The thought came to him that if he had ever found himself in the same situation as Rob, he would have acted in the same way.

'If you're going to stand any chance at all,' he said, 'you need to be trained by an expert. And I just had an idea. As a general rule, I don't like bounty hunters. But there's one called Will Cartwright who's different from the rest. He helped save my life once when I'd been ambushed by a gang of outlaws. I found out later that his parents had died in a cholera epidemic when he was still a baby, and he'd been brought up in a big orphanage in Texas. I never got to find out how he came to be a bounty hunter, but I do know that most of the reward money he was getting went to help run the orphanage he was brought up in.

'Will's too old for bounty hunting now, and he lives in a shack on the outskirts of Cheyenne. When you've settled up here, come to see me in Cheyenne, and if we haven't captured the Nolan gang by then, I'll take you to see Cartwright. Maybe he'll agree to take you in hand. In his day, he was a top class gunfighter. And his record of rewards received speaks for itself.'

Rob thanked the marshal and said he would do as Winter suggested. Then the marshal rode off.

Two days later, Nelson's brother Jake turned up with his wife and child: Nelson brought him to see Rob, and Jake jumped at the chance of taking over the Sinclair homestead. A price was agreed, and Rob asked Carter at the bank to arrange for the legal formalities to be completed as quickly as possible Twenty days later, he and Elizabeth were ready to leave for Cheyenne.

When they arrived there, in the evening, they went straight to the general store owned by Jed Baxter, the husband of their Aunt Sarah. Their arrival was expected. The store was closed, and they all sat in the living quarters. Jed was a short, energetic man, who, with his wife's help, had built up a substantial business at the store. Sarah, also short, was plump and vivacious. The couple were childless, a fact which had caused them great disappointment.

'That was a terrible thing that happened on the homestead,' said Sarah.

'We want you to know that Elizabeth is very welcome to live here with us. She can help us out in the store. And you're welcome to stay here yourself, Rob, if that's what you want. We've got plenty of room.'

'We're real obliged to you both for taking care of Elizabeth,' said Rob. 'As for myself, I'd like to stay a short while, but if the law hasn't caught up with the Nolan gang, I'll be going after them. I'll go see the US marshal in the morning, if he's in town, to check on the situation.'

Sarah and her husband exchanged glances.

'I know the marshal's in town,' said Jed, 'but are you sure this is really what you want to do?'

'I'm sure,' Rob replied. 'I know it's dangerous, but it's something I've got to do. And my mind just ain't for changing.'

The following morning Rob went to see Marshal Winter, who told him that two days after the bank robbery in Winslow the gang had been spotted, by a homesteader, as they were crossing the border into Kansas. Then they vanished without a trace. A posse in Kansas tried to pick up their trail, but it was hopeless.

'Are you still set on going after the gang?' asked Winter.

'Yes, I am,' said Rob, 'and I'm looking forward to meeting up with Mr Cartwright.'

'I've spoken with Will already,' said the marshal, 'and he said he don't mind looking you over to see if he can make a fighting man out of you. Between you and me, I got the feeling that he's finding life a mite boring nowadays, after all those years of chasing the outlaws. I'll take you along to see him now.'

Winter walked with Rob to the edge of town and stopped outside a small shack. He knocked on the door, which was opened by Cartwright, who let them in. He was a bearded, stocky man in his sixties, still keen of eye and light on his feet. He looked Rob over.

'This is Rob Sinclair,' said the marshal. 'The one who's itching to go after the Nolan gang. I'm going to leave you two to get better acquainted.'

After Winter's departure, Rob shifted uneasily on his feet as Cartwright looked him up and down, then walked around him to study him from various angles, before returning to face him.

'It's not going to be an easy job,' he said, 'and it's going to take time. But I suppose we can have a try. I'll tell you the weapons you need to buy. You don't want anything fancy. Get a Colt Peacemaker .45 with a seven and a half inch barrel, and an 1873 model Winchester .44–.40 rifle. And buy plenty of ammunition.'

'I'm obliged to you for helping me out,' said Rob. 'I've got the money to pay you for your time.'

'I don't want no pay,' said Cartwright. 'You go and buy those two weapons and ammunition, and come back here early this afternoon. No need to buy a gun belt and holster. I happen to have a spare one that'll suit you fine. The holster's just right for the Colt you're going to buy. I had it made special for myself. I guess you're naturally right-handed?'

Rob confirmed this, and departed. When he returned later in the day he was carrying the six-gun and rifle, with suitable ammunition. Cartwright examined the weapons closely.

'They'll do,' he said. 'Now you've got to understand that a few things need attention before a man stands any chance of getting to be a real expert with a six-gun. Take the gun belt and holster for example. The exact location of the holster depends on the length of a man's arm. It should be located so that just after the hand has started moving upwards it can close on the handle of the gun and pull it upwards out of the holster. And it goes without saying that the gun must be a smooth, easy fit in the holster. A fraction of a second's delay in pulling a six-gun out could mean the difference between life and death if you're facing a top gunfighter.'

He told Rob to strap on the gun belt and let his hand hang loosely by his side.

'The holster needs to be a mite lower,' he said. 'I'll fix that right now.'

When he had done this, he dropped the Colt .45 into the holster. Then he buckled on a gun belt and holster himself and, using his own six-gun, he went through the motions of raising his hand, taking hold of the handle of the six-gun, pulling it out of the holster, and levelling it, all in one smooth, continuous movement. He repeated this several times, then told Rob to follow

his example. Rob drew his own gun several times.

'Not near as smooth as it needs to be,' said Cartwright. 'And your hand has got to know exactly where that gun handle is, without any need for you to look down at it. Your eyes need to be on the man you're drawing against.'

He told Rob to pull the gun out another twenty times.

'That's more like it,' he said, when Rob had finished, 'but there's a long way to go yet. For the rest of the afternoon, you'd better practise this part of the draw. You need to get it right before we move on to the cocking, aiming and pulling the trigger.'

When Rob went to the shack the following morning, he continued for a while, under his tutor's watchful eye, to practise the move he had been working on the previous day. Then Cartwright, using an unloaded gun, demonstrated to him how to introduce the pulling back of the hammer while still maintaining a

smooth continuous movement of the weapon.

'As for aiming the gun,' he told Rob, 'you just point it at the spot you want your bullet to hit. And after a lot of target practice, which we'll come to later, you should end up pointing it in exactly the right direction. And that's just as important as making a fast draw, which ain't much use if the bullet misses its target. For the rest of the day carry on practising what you've just seen me doing, and I'll let you know if you're doing anything wrong. Don't bother too much about speed at first. That'll come with practice.'

On the following day, Rob continued to practise his draw, and during an interval Cartwright showed him how to take his six-gun to pieces, clean and oil it, and reassemble it. At the end of the day, he told Rob that on the following day they would walk a little way out of town for some target practice.

The next morning they walked to a small group of trees about a mile from

the edge of town. They were carrying their six-guns and a supply of ammunition. Rob was also carrying a large number of sheets of stiff white paper, which he had purchased and cut down to size in accordance with Cartwright's instructions.

Cartwright selected a large tree with a broad trunk, and tacked a sheet of paper on it about four feet from the ground. Then he marked a line on the ground eight paces from the base of the tree. Telling Rob to watch closely, he loaded his six-gun, stood on the line, and in six fluid movements, he made six successive draws with the single-action weapon, firing a bullet at the target each time. Then he and Rob walked up to the target. In the centre of it were six bullet holes, two of them slightly overlapping.

'My sight ain't as good as it used to be,' said Cartwright, 'and maybe I could have done a little better than that when I was younger. But as far as accuracy goes, if you can end up with a result like that, you can be satisfied. Now it's your turn. And always remember that speed is important, but not at the expense of accuracy. And another thing. Shooting at a target is a whole lot different than shooting at a man. You won't know how you'll react until it actually happens.'

Rob started shooting at the target, changing the paper after each six shots, and handing it to the man watching him. When he had fired twenty-four shots, Cartwright spoke to him.

'Your movements are all OK,' he said, 'but as you can see, more often than not, you're missing the target. Practice should help with that. I want you to carry on like this on your own for the next few days. Come and tell me when you're getting the same sort of result I got earlier myself.'

Three days later, Rob called at the shack in the morning, and he and Cartwright walked to the place where Rob had been practising. Cartwright tacked a target on to a tree not far from the one Rob had been using before. Immediately above this target paper he tacked three more, and below it, a further two. He walked back eight paces, and as Rob joined him they saw Marshal Winter, riding towards town, turn and head in their direction. They waited until he dismounted and walked up to them. Winter saw the targets on the tree trunk. He smiled at Rob and his companion.

'I've been wondering, Will,' he said, 'just how far you've got in making a fighting man out of young Rob here.'

'You've come just at the right time,' said Cartwright. 'He was just going to show me how he's shaping up as a gunfighter. Carry on, Rob. Make six draws on my call, and fire one shot at each of the targets for each draw.'

With two critical pairs of eyes watching him closely, Rob turned to face the targets, and stood nicely balanced, awaiting Cartwright's first call. When it came, the two onlookers were greatly impressed by Rob's instant response and the eye-defeating rapidity of his draw right up to the time that the bullet was discharged. Doubtful as to whether such speed could be combined with accuracy, they waited while Rob fired at the remaining five targets, then walked up to the tree with him.

They both stared at the six targets. Each one of them was marked by a bullet hole within half an inch of its centre. The marshal looked at Cartwright.

'Seems like you've done a real good job, Will,' he said. 'That is *some* shooting.'

'Even in my prime,' said Cartwright, 'I never done better than this, and maybe not as good. We'll do some work on moving targets, then we'll start on the Winchester.'

Two days later the instruction on the use of the Winchester rifle began. Cartwright told Rob that the weapon was accurate for distances of up to 200 yards at least, when the extra rear sight was used. He explained the technique to be used when firing at moving targets, and how to allow for the effect of wind. After three days of tuition had been completed, Cartwright expressed himself satisfied with Rob's performance.

'As far as handling a six-gun and a rifle are concerned,' he said, 'you've reached a pretty high standard. High enough to give you just a slim chance, maybe, of getting the better of Nolan and his gang. Another thing that could help is for you to learn how to follow sign. It takes years of experience to make an expert tracker, and nobody can beat the Indians at it. They can spot and read sign that a white man would never notice. All the same, I can teach you a few things about it that could be useful. But we need to ride out of town for a few days.'

Three days later they returned to Cartwright's shack, with Rob much more confident about his tracking ability.

'I reckon you're ready to start out

now,' said Cartwright, 'but don't forget to keep up your shooting practice. Your problem now is how are you going to find the Nolan gang? I know nothing about them myself. I reckon the best thing you could do is . . . ' He stopped as he heard a knock on the door. The caller was Marshal Winter. Cartwright invited him in.

'Just got some news about the Nolan gang,' said Winter. 'Figured Rob here would be interested. They robbed a stagecoach two days ago in the Texas Panhandle, north of Amarillo. There were only three robbers, but the leader was definitely identified as Nolan. The stage was carrying a strongbox. They took the contents and crossed the border into the Indian Territory a long way ahead of the posse that set out after them. They left the shotgun rider dead.'

He handed Rob copies of WANTED posters showing the faces of the four men in the gang, and told him that it was thought that the missing member of the gang was Turner. The US marshal in Fort Smith, Arkansas, whose deputies patrolled the Indian Territory, had been told that the gang had moved into his territory.

'If you go to Amarillo,' said Winter, 'the US marshal there, name of Kennedy, knows from me that you're aiming to go after the Nolan gang. He'll tell you anything you want to know about the robbery. The rest will be up to you.'

Thanking Cartwright and the marshal, Rob said that he would set off for Amarillo in the morning. Then he went to the store for a talk with Elizabeth.

'I'll be leaving tomorrow,' he said. 'Are you happy here, Elizabeth?'

She nodded her head. 'I like helping out in the store,' she said.

'That's good,' said Rob. 'I don't know how long I'll be away. When I come back, we'll start thinking about what we want to do with our lives.'

Rob went to see the storekeeper and his wife. He told them that he was leaving the following day.

'We guess it's no good trying to change your mind,' said Jed Baxter, 'so we'll just wish you well.'

'Don't worry about Elizabeth,' said Sarah. 'We both really like having her here. She's a good girl. Helps us in the store quite a lot. Seems to like doing it.'

The following morning Rob boarded the stage for Amarillo.

3

Rob arrived in Amarillo just after noon. He took a room at the hotel in the centre of town and had a meal. Then he went to see US Marshal Kennedy in his office. He introduced himself to the marshal. Kennedy, an alert, competent-looking officer in his early fifties, regarded Rob with interest.

'Marshal Winter told me about you,' he said. 'I can tell you that once again the Nolan gang has got away with it. The law has heard of no sightings of them since the robbery. As far as the robbery is concerned, they held up a stagecoach seventeen miles north of Amarillo, that's about five miles past the first swing station from here. The shotgun rider was killed, and the driver injured so bad that he couldn't drive on.

'The posse managed to track them to

the border with the Indian Territory, and I notified the US marshal in Fort Smith of this. We've heard nothing back from him since, but I know he's short of deputies, and my guess is that the gang has not been picked up, and has gone into hiding somewhere in the territory.'

'Would there be any chance of following their tracks from the border?' asked Rob.

'No chance at all,' replied Kennedy. 'I know for a fact that the trail they were riding along has been used since by a string of freight wagons heading east. I know why you want to see the Nolan gang brought to justice, but I can't think of any way you can find out where they are.'

Rob thanked the marshal and went back to his hotel room to consider his next move. He remembered Cartwright telling him that when a stagecoach robbery was being planned, it was not unusual for the gang to hide out some place not far from the spot where the robbery was to take place. He decided to hire a mount and ride out the following day to the location of the hold-up. Then he would search for a possible hideout. If this was discovered, there was just the slimmest of chances that it might yield some useful information which would help him in his search for the gang.

When he arrived there the following morning he saw the tracks made by the posse as they set off after the outlaws. He rode north for a mile, then circled the scene of the robbery, looking, without success for the tracks of three horses leading towards it. Then he rode out a further half mile and repeated the process. This time he was successful. He had only ridden half a mile when, on a small patch of ground which was soft, and almost bare, he spotted the tracks of three horses.

The tracks were coming from the direction of a distant ridge to the north-west, and Rob headed for this. Halfway there, he decided to investigate a gully ahead of him, slightly to the left. He entered it, and rode along the bottom. It soon became apparent that the gully had been recently occupied by men and horses. He stopped at the point where a campfire had been set up, and dismounted. Carefully, he examined the site. It was clear that it was not more than a few days since it had been vacated. Rob was reasonably sure that he had found the Nolan gang's hideout. He took another careful look around, but could find nothing to help him in his search for the robbers. Disappointed, he mounted his horse. About to ride off, his eye was caught by something white poking out from underneath a stone at the edge of the remains of the campfire.

He dismounted and carefully removed the stone, to reveal a charred piece of paper which broke up as he removed it, leaving only a small unburnt portion between his fingers. He studied this carefully. On it, faint and barely readable, were sixteen letters, near to the end of what looked like a telegraph message. These were: SOUTH OF BRODY. TURN. Looking at them, it occurred to Rob that the last word in the message could have been TURNER, the message having been sent by him to Nolan. As for the word BRODY, this could, he thought, be the name of a place.

He rode back to Amarillo and went to see Marshal Kennedy. He showed him the scrap of paper he had found in the gully, and suggested that the unfinished word might have been TURNER. He asked the marshal if he knew of a place called Brody.

'Only one I know of,' replied Kennedy, 'and that's in the north of the Indian Territory, south of Dodge, near the Kansas border. I'm guessing you were right, thinking that Turner sent that message to Nolan. Maybe they were going to meet in Brody after the robbery. Maybe they were planning to hide out together somewhere near there. Or perhaps by now, they've all left. Or it could be that none of these

41

guesses is right.'

'I'm going to ride to Brody,' said Rob, 'and see if I can get on their trail.'

Kennedy wished him luck, and Rob went to the nearby livery stable to buy a horse. He mentioned that he was heading for Brody the following morning.

'Would that be the Brody in the Indian Territory, south of Dodge, or the one in Texas, a long way south of here, not far from Fort Worth?' asked the livery-man. 'I've heard of the first, the second one I passed through once, on a stagecoach.'

'The first one is the one I was aiming to visit,' said Rob.

He selected a good-looking chestnut horse from the ones shown to him. On the ride to his destination there would be plenty of time for him and his mount to get acquainted, as well as time for some shooting practice.

But as he walked back to the hotel, the thought came to him that Nolan and the others could have ridden into

Indian Territory just to get rid of the following posse, and could then have turned south to head for the Brody near Fort Worth. Which one should he head for? He settled it by tossing a coin, and the following morning, wearing his Colt Peacemaker, and with the Winchester in a saddle holster and a bedroll tied behind the saddle, he rode off south through the Texas Panhandle.

He reached the end of a long uneventful journey in the early afternoon. Walking his horse down the dusty main street, he passed the hotel and general store, before reaching the livery stable opposite the saloon. He stopped outside it and dismounted. Looking along the street, he saw a young woman riding towards him from the south end of town. He guessed she was around his own age. She was a slim, attractive woman with auburn hair, wearing a Texas hat and smart riding clothes. She glanced at Rob as she passed. She stopped at the store and went inside. Two men who had come out of the saloon just after she passed it stood on the boardwalk watching her until she disappeared from view. Each of them was wearing a six-gun in a right-hand holster. One of the men said something to his companion and they both laughed. Then someone called to them from inside the saloon, and they both went back in.

From just inside the stable, Randle, the liveryman, saw Rob's arrival, and also the young woman and the two men outside the saloon. He came out to speak to Rob.

'Howdy,' said Rob. 'I'd be obliged if you'd feed and water my horse. We've had a long ride. I figure to stay here maybe a day or two.'

'Sure,' said the liveryman. 'I can see you're a stranger round here, so let me give you a word of warning. Those two men you just saw go back into the saloon are Donovan and Fletcher. They work on the big Circle Dot Ranch. They're just plain ornery, and fancy themselves as gunfighters. I'd steer well clear of them if I were you.'

'Thanks for the warning,' said Rob. 'I don't aim to look for trouble. Who was the young lady?'

'That's Marian Lee,' said Randle. 'Her father runs the small Crazy L spread next to the Circle Dot. And Vickery, that's the owner of the Circle Dot, is set on buying him out. But Lee just ain't interested.'

Rob decided to go and take a room at the hotel, after calling at the general store for a new razor which he needed. He took his leave of the liveryman and walked to the store. Inside were Marian Lee and the elderly storekeeper, Bellamy, and his wife. They all glanced at him as he came in. Bellamy was attending to Marian. His wife moved along the counter to serve Rob. She showed him some razors and he selected one. As he was waiting for his change, Marian completed her purchase and walked out of the store.

When Rob followed her shortly after, she was standing on the boardwalk facing Donovan and Fletcher who had blocked her way as she was walking towards her horse. Rob stopped behind her.

'What do you two men want?' she asked, angrily.

'We was just aiming to give you some good advice to pass on to your father,' said Donovan, a burly man in his late twenties, with an arrogant look about him. 'Tell him that Mr Vickery's getting mighty tired of waiting for him to take up his offer for the Crazy L. He needs that range. He ain't going to wait much longer for your father to make up his mind.'

'Is that a threat?' asked Marian. 'Can't Vickery get it into his stupid head that the Crazy L is not for sale. Let me pass.'

Grinning, the two men made no move to do as she asked. They looked closely at Rob as he walked up and stood at Marian's side. He had felt compelled to help her, and he realized that his gunfighting skills, and his ability to deal with human targets, was probably about to be tested. Calmly, he spoke to the two men in front of him.

'You heard the lady,' he said. 'Better do like she says.'

The two men looked hard at the youthful Rob. Then Donovan's temper flared.

'This ain't no business of yours, mister,' he said. 'If you want to stay healthy, you'll pick up your horse and ride straight out of town.'

'I aim to stay here as long as I need to,' said Rob, then spoke to the girl beside him without taking his eyes off the two Circle Dot hands.

'I'd be obliged, miss,' he said, 'if you'd step inside the store, so I can stop these two bullies from hassling you.'

Marian looked at him, and hesitated for a moment. Then, reluctantly, she walked back into the store. She went to the window looking out on to the street. Curious, the storekeeper and his wife joined her.

'I want you two to move off this

boardwalk and ride out of town,' said Rob. He was aware that a gun battle was probably imminent, but after his tuition at the hands of Cartwright, he was confident of the outcome.

Donovan, with Fletcher standing by his side, spoke angrily.

'You had your chance to leave,' he said. 'Now let's see how handy you are with that six-gun of yours.'

He made the fast draw which was the envy of his fellow ranch hands on the Circle Dot, and which he was confident would take care of this meddlesome stranger. But Rob's Peacemaker appeared miraculously in his right hand, and he shot Donovan's six-gun from his grasp before the weapon had been levelled. Re-cocked, the Peacemaker was pointing at Fletcher before he realized that his confidence in Donovan's ability to take care of the stranger had been misplaced.

'I wouldn't,' shouted Rob, as Fletcher, similar in size and age to his companion, grabbed the handle of his six-gun. Fletcher froze, realizing that he stood no chance of firing first. Then, at Rob's command, he lifted his six-gun out of the holster, and dropped it on the board-walk. Fuming, he and Donovan, who was nursing a damaged right hand, stood looking at the barrel of Rob's Peace-maker.

'Time to leave town,' said Rob. 'Leave your guns where they are. You can collect them next time you come into town.'

'You'll be sorry you ever came to Brody,' said Donovan. Then he and his partner turned, walked to their horses, and rode out of town to the south. Their departure was watched by a small group of townspeople, including the liveryman, who had observed the incident. Rob picked up the guns and went back into the store. He spoke to Marian, who had witnessed the encounter.

'I'm glad to say, miss,' he said, 'that I managed to persuade those two bullies to leave town.'

'I'm obliged for what you did,' said Marian, 'but I saw how you handled those two, and I'm sure they won't let it rest. Neither will Josh Vickery, the owner of the Circle Dot. He's an arrogant man. Thinks he can ride roughshod over the folks around here. If you're wise, you'll leave town right now.'

'Can't do that,' said Rob. 'I've some business to tend to here. The name's Rob Sinclair, by the way.'

'Marian Lee,' she said, thinking that this was a man she could take a liking to if she ever got the chance, and feeling concern about the danger he would be in if he stayed around. 'I sure hope that business don't take too long.'

As Rob left the store, she moved to the window and watched him as he walked to the hotel and went inside.

4

In the hotel lobby, Rob found the liveryman talking to Hilton, the hotel owner. As Rob came in, they broke off their conversation, and turned to face him. The livery man spoke.

'By now,' he said, 'the whole town's talking about the way you cut Donovan and Fletcher down to size. And it sure did pleasure them to see or hear about what happened. Folks are just plain fed up with the way they and some other Circle Dot hands behave in town. And it don't do no good to speak to Vickery about it.'

'I reckon you'd better think twice about staying on here,' said Hilton, a short, dapper man with a neat black moustache. 'Vickery might take this as personal and send some men after you. There's no law officer in town.'

Rob judged that he could take the

two men into his confidence.

'I'm here for a reason,' he said. From his pocket he pulled a folded copy of a wanted poster with Turner's picture on it. He unfolded it and showed it to the two men.

'Has either of you seen this man recently?' he asked.

Randle's reply was almost immediate. '*I've* seen him,' he said. 'He came to the stable, maybe a week ago, with Walton, ramrod of the Circle Dot. He was looking to buy a horse, but I had nothing to suit him. I'd never seen him before, and I ain't seen him in town since. If he's wanted by the law, I'm wondering what he was doing at the Circle Dot.'

'I'm wondering the same thing,' said Rob, as he took from his pocket the wanted posters for Nolan and the other two members of the gang. He showed them to Hilton and Randle. He asked if they had seen any of the three. Both men, after a close study of the pictures, shook their heads.

'Like the posters say,' said Rob, 'all four are members of the Nolan gang of outlaws, wanted for multiple robbery and murder. I'd like to tell you just why I'm here, but I need your word that you'll keep the information to yourselves.'

'You have it,' said the liveryman, and Hilton nodded agreement. Rob then told them about the murder of his parents by the gang, and of his determination to bring Nolan and the others to justice. He showed them the piece of charred paper which had brought him to Brody.

'Before I bring the law in,' he said, 'I need to find out whether Turner's still around here, and whether Nolan and the others have joined him. Maybe they're all hiding out at the Circle Dot.'

'Could be,' said Randle, 'but how are you going to find out? The only visitors allowed on the Circle Dot are ones invited by Vickery himself.'

'Looks like I'll have to ride in during the night, then,' said Rob, 'and see if I

53

can spot the gang there while it's dark.'

'It's a big risk you'll be taking,' said Hilton. 'It's clear from what happened here today that you can take care of yourself, but you'll be facing a lot of guns on the Circle Dot.'

'It's a risk I'll have to take,' said Rob. 'Has either of you ever been there?'

'I have,' said the liveryman. 'Just once, a while back. Vickery asked me to go out there to take a look at a sick horse.'

'In that case,' said Rob, 'I'd be obliged if you'd tell me about the location of the ranch, and the size and layout of the buildings.'

When Randle had done this, Rob thanked him and told the two men that he would leave after dark on the following day, and would return to Brody before daybreak. Then he signed the hotel register and Hilton gave him the key to his room.

He stayed there till supper time, then went down to the hotel dining room for a meal. He had just finished this, and was about to leave, when a man came in and walked up to his table.

'My name's Walton, ramrod on the Circle Dot,' he said. 'I'd like a few words with you.'

Rob motioned to an empty chair, and Walton sat down on it. He was a big man, well dressed, and a little over-weight.

'Mr Vickery asked me to bring a message to you,' he said. 'First of all, he don't bear no grudge over the way you handled Donovan and Fletcher. It's time they were taught a lesson. He wants you to come out to the ranch to see him. He's got a proposition to put to you. Reckons maybe it's one you can't turn down. You can ride back with me if it suits you.'

Rob couldn't believe his luck. He now had the chance of visiting the Circle Dot openly, with the possible chance of establishing whether or not the Nolan gang was there. He arranged to meet Walton at the livery stable half an hour later.

After Walton had left the hotel, Rob told Hilton what had happened. He gave him the four wanted posters to hide in a safe place. He said he would return from the ranch later in the day. When he went to the stable for his horse, he had time, before Walton turned up, to tell the liveryman of the message from Vickery.

'It could be a trap, of course,' he said, 'but I don't think so. I'll see you when I get back.'

Walton turned up a few minutes later, and Rob rode with him to the Circle Dot buildings, about six miles south of town. They were just as Randle had described them — mainly a large house with ground and first floors, bunkhouse, cookshack and barn. A few hands were standing near the bunkhouse, all strangers to Rob. They looked at him curiously as he rode up to the house with the ramrod and dismounted. Walton led him inside.

Vickery, seated at a desk at one end of the large living room, rose as the two men came in. He was a short man in his fifties, strongly built, with a head large in proportion to the rest of his body. Keen eyes studied Rob from under a pair of beetle brows. He invited him and Walton to sit down.

'From what I was told by two of my hands,' he said, 'you rate pretty high as a gunfighter. Seems like they made a bad mistake when they hassled you.'

'All I wanted to do was walk along the boardwalk,' said Rob. 'All they had to do was get out of my way.'

'I have a friend,' said Vickery, 'who's looking hard for a top gun. He ain't here now, but I expect him before long. If you join up with him, and don't mind breaking the law now and then, he can make you a rich man. Have you ever been in trouble with the law?'

'Maybe,' said Rob.

'About that shooting in town,' said Vickery. 'To shoot a gun out of a man's hand in the middle of a draw takes some doing. Is that what you was actually aiming to do, or was it just chance?'

'I was aiming to shoot the gun out of the man's hand,' said Rob.

'In that case,' said Vickery, 'if you don't mind, I'd sure admire to see you in action.'

'Sure,' said Rob. 'What d'you have in mind?'

Picking up a bag, the rancher led the way to the fence surrounding a small corral. From the bag he took nails, a hammer and six small thin circular discs of tin. He nailed the discs, in a vertical position, at intervals along the side of the top rail. Then he walked back from the rail and marked a line on the ground. He returned to Rob.

'What I'd like you to do,' he said, 'if you have a mind, is draw on my call, and fire two shots at two of those targets as quick as you can. Then do the same for another two, and the same for the last pair.'

Rob walked to the line on the ground and turned to face the fence. On Vickery's call, the smoothness of the instant draw, and the rapidity with which two shots were fired at the targets, greatly impressed the onlookers, among whom were several ranch hands. To avoid ending up with an empty gun, Rob replaced the two spent cartridges before firing two more shots. Then, after reloading, he fired a further two at the targets.

Vickery and Walton, followed by Rob, walked up to the fence and inspected the targets one by one. In each case the bullet had passed through the thin disc close to its centre. The rancher turned to Rob.

'I reckon I'd go a long way to see better shooting than that,' he said. 'I've no doubt at all you're just the man my friend's looking for.'

'Does your friend have a name?' asked Rob.

'You'll find that out if and when you join up with him,' said Vickery. 'Does the proposition interest you? If it does, you can move here if you like, and wait till he turns up.'

'I'm going back to Brody now,' said

Rob. 'I'll think on it and let you know.'

As Rob rode off a few minutes later, he saw several ranch hands standing at the fence looking at the perforated targets. On his way to Brody, he decided to return to the ranch the following day to await the arrival of Vickery's friend. There was, he thought, a chance that this friend was either Turner or Nolan.

When he arrived at Brody, he stopped at the livery stable to hand over his horse. He told Randle what had happened at the Circle Dot, and of his intention to move in there the following day. As he finished speaking, a fast-moving rider raced into town, and slid to a stop outside the house of Doc Fender, adjacent to the livery stable. The rider dismounted and ran to the door of the house. He knocked on it urgently.

'That's Luke Warner, one of the Crazy L hands,' said the liveryman. 'Looks like somebody's in trouble.'

The knocks were not answered, and

Warner ran to the stable.

'Mark Lee's hurt bad,' he told Randle. 'He was hit by rifle fire. You any idea where I'll find Doc Fender?'

'Try the saloon,' said Randle. 'Sometimes he goes in there around this time.'

Warner ran to the saloon, and came out almost immediately with the doctor. Fender was a slender man, in his early sixties, bearded and neatly dressed. He was highly respected in the community. As he hurried towards his house, he called out to Randle to hitch up his buggy. Warner helped the liveryman to do this, as Rob stood by. He told them that Lee had been shot from ambush by an unknown rifleman while checking some sick cows, and had lain unconscious for a while before being discovered.

'You got any idea who was behind this?' asked the liveryman.

'We're pretty sure that would be Vickery of the Circle Dot,' said Warner, 'but we ain't got no proof.'

As he finished speaking, the doctor hurried up with his medical bag, and a moment later, accompanied by Warner on his horse, he drove the buggy towards the Crazy L. When they had left, Rob asked Randle how many hands worked on the Crazy L. The liveryman told him that there were two, Warner and a man called Hank Garner. Both men had been with Lee for a long time, and although getting on in years, were still pretty spry.

'I think I'll ride out to the Crazy L,' said Rob, 'and see if I can lend them a hand while Lee's out of action.'

'I reckon they'd be glad of it,' said Randle, 'but what about that proposition Vickery put to you?'

'Vickery's friend, whoever that might be, ain't due here for a while,' said Rob, 'and in any case, I reckon that giving help to Lee comes first. I'll have a quick meal, then ride out there.'

Later on, as Rob took a meal at the hotel, he reflected on how much he had matured since first meeting Cartwright, the old bounty hunter. Apart from imparting his gunfighting skills to Rob, the old man had described many of his pursuits of outlaws and his confrontations with them. Rob had learnt much from these accounts, and his confidence that he could bring the Nolan gang to justice had been boosted.

5

Two hours after Doc Fender and Warner had left town, Rob rode off towards the Crazy L, following directions given him by the liveryman. A mile short of his destination he met Doc Fender, returning to Brody. He asked Fender how seriously Lee had been injured.

'Pretty bad,' said the doctor. 'He had a rifle bullet in the back. I've taken it out, and I don't think any serious damage has been done. But he'll need to stay in bed for two weeks at least, while the wound heals. I'm calling at the ranch tomorrow to see how he's doing. Are you heading for the Crazy L now?'

'I am,' said Rob. 'I figured maybe they could do with some help.'

'You figured right,' said the doctor. 'I could tell that Marian's pretty worried about the situation. Seeing as how you helped her out in town, I reckon she'll be mighty glad to see you.'

They parted company, and Rob rode on to the ranch. The two hands, standing outside the small bunkhouse, walked up to him as he stopped outside the house. The door opened, and Marian stepped out. She looked surprised to see him.

'Howdy,' said Rob. 'I rode out figuring you might need some help. Passed the doctor on the way. He told me about your father.'

'Help is what we need,' said Marian, 'help to stand up to Vickery and his men. And from the way you tamed Donovan and Fletcher the other day, we couldn't hope for anyone better than yourself. But I don't know that we could pay your price.'

'I wasn't aiming to be paid,' said Rob. 'Food and a place to sleep is all I want.'

'We'll have to speak to my father,' said Marian. 'But not now. He's dozing,

65

and very weak. Maybe tomorrow. We have a spare bedroom in the house. You can use that.'

Accompanied by the two hands, Rob and Marian went into the house to discuss the situation.

'Hank and Luke here,' said Marian, after introducing the two hands to Rob, 'are just as keen as Father and I to hold on to the Crazy L.'

'I reckon it's time I told you just why I came to Brody,' said Rob, 'but I'd be obliged if you'd keep the information to yourselves. Apart from the hotel keeper and the liveryman in Brody, nobody knows my real reason for being here.'

He went on to tell them of his search for the Nolan gang and the reason for it. He showed them the four wanted posters, which he had brought with him, and told them that Turner had been seen in town with the ramrod of the Circle Dot.

'I don't know where the gang is now,' he said, 'but I'm hoping they'll turn up here soon. But the main thing now is to stop Vickery from taking over the Crazy L. I don't know much about raising cows, so Hank and Luke can show me what needs to be done. And maybe I can help in stopping any of us getting killed, now that Vickery's started to play rough. I reckon the first thing to do is set up a night guard to warn of anybody sneaking up on us in the dark. Me and Hank and Luke could take it in turns to be on watch. My guess is that Vickery's men will be aiming to do their dirty work without being seen and recognized. What weapons have you on the Crazy L?'

'Me and Luke both have an old Colt .45,' said Hank. 'They mostly stay in the bunkhouse, and I don't remember the last time they were fired.'

'In the house here, we have a six-gun and a Winchester rifle with a small amount of ammunition,' said Marian.

'I'll ride into town tomorrow for a good supply of ammunition,' said Rob. 'As for tonight, I reckon it's unlikely they'll strike again so soon, but in case they do we need to be ready for them. The night guard on duty outside the house needs to be able to alert the other two immediately if he sees or hears intruders. Let's take a look outside.'

They went out, and Rob looked at the walkway, open on one side, which led from the bunkhouse to a second door into the house, this opening on to the kitchen. Here the meals, prepared by Marian, were taken by the rancher and his daughter and the two hands.

'Just outside the kitchen door,' said Rob, 'would be a good place for the guard to stand. He'd have a little cover there. And he'd be near to the window in the walkway. He'd have to be able to alert the other two inside to join him. Where's the spare bedroom?'

'Right over the kitchen,' said Marian.

'Good,' said Rob. 'What we need then are two lengths of strong twine, passing through staples half driven into the timber. One would run from inside the walkway to the spare bedroom. The other would run from the same place to the bunkhouse. Inside the bedroom and the bunkhouse, something would be rigged up so that a pull on the cord by the guard would set up enough disturbance to waken a sleeping man. That's how I see it. But maybe one of you has a better idea?'

They all shook their heads, and Rob and the two hands set to and installed the alarm system as suggested by Rob. When this had been done they made sure that all door and window fastenings were in good order.

The night passed without incident, and after breakfast Marian took Rob to see her father. Mark Lee was in his middle fifties, a big man, strong and resolute, still mourning the loss of his wife in a cholera epidemic twelve months earlier. When they entered the bedroom, he was half sitting up on the bed, his face drawn and his back supported by pillows. He studied Rob's face closely before speaking in a faint voice.

'I reckon I've been hit bad, Sinclair,' he said, 'but I ain't finished yet. Marian told me why you're here, and I'm obliged for your help. I never figured that Vickery would go so far as to have me shot down, but I guess I was wrong. It's clear he's dead set on taking over the Crazy L. I reckon we're in real trouble, with no law nearby to call on, and no certain proof that somebody from the Circle Dot put that rifle bullet in me. There ain't much more we can do but look after the cattle, and watch out for trouble, day and night. I ain't much use myself right now, but Doc Fender says I should be out of bed in a week or so, and ready to ride maybe a couple of weeks later.'

'Me and the hands'll keep things running,' said Rob. 'And I aim to help guard you all from any danger from the Circle Dot. Now I'm going to ride into Brody for some ammunition. I'll be back as soon as I can.'

★　★　★

Late in the afternoon, on the day after the shooting of Mark Lee, a Circle Dot hand rode back to the ranch from town to give Vickery the news that Lee was still alive and expected to recover, and that the stranger Sinclair was helping out on the Crazy L. A little later, Vickery discussed the situation with Walton, his ramrod.

'It's bad news,' he said. 'First, that rifle shot should've been fatal. And second, it looks like Sinclair's turned down my offer and has joined up with Lee. The first thing we've got to do is get rid of Sinclair. Then we can deal with the others. I think I'll hire Sweeney to do the job. I heard from Nolan that right now he's in his usual hideout just inside the Indian Territory. That's less than a day's ride from here. Leave early in the morning, and bring him back as soon as you can.'

Walton rode off at daybreak the following day, and returned with Sweeney late in the evening of the next day. Sweeney was a short man, powerfully built, with a swarthy, impassive face and beetling eyebrows. He was well known to the criminal fraternity and the law as a ruthless killer whose gun was for hire if the price was right. He always worked alone and was relentless in the pursuit of his quarry. Walton took him into the living room where Vickery was waiting. They all sat down.

'This man Sinclair you want me to get rid of,' said Sweeney. 'What d'you know about him?'

'Not a lot,' replied Vickery. 'He's a stranger in these parts. He's pretty young, and he's handy with a six-gun, which is why I called you in. You know that Nolan's looking for another man to join his gang. I sounded Sinclair out about this, but it didn't come to nothing.'

Vickery went on to give Sweeney detailed information about the Crazy L and the people living there.

'This looks like a straightforward job,' said Sweeney. 'Nobody at the

Crazy L knows me, and they don't know I'm working for you. I'll ride there tomorrow and tend to Sinclair. From what you tell me, Lee's out of action, but are the two hands liable to give me any trouble?'

'I doubt it,' said Vickery. 'They're both getting on in years. Just finish Sinclair off, and leave the others for me to tend to later. Now, if you go to the cookshack, I'll get the cook to rustle up a meal for you. And there's a bedroom in the house you can use.'

'Right,' said Sweeney. 'After supper I'll work out a plan for tomorrow.'

★　★　★

On the day after Sweeney's arrival at the Circle Dot, Rob took breakfast in the house. Marian told him that her father had slept a while during the night, and his wound seemed to be healing well.

'He don't take kindly to being laid up with the ranch under threat,' she said.

'D'you think we can expect more trouble soon?'

'It's hard to say,' Rob replied, ignorant of the fact that trouble was already on its way.

He and the hands had decided that for the time being they would not ride out on to the range, but would attend to the chores in and around the buildings. They were so engaged when Luke Warner noticed a plume of dense smoke rising from behind a low ridge over half a mile east of the ranch house. He drew it to the attention of the others.

'There's some brush on the far side of that ridge,' he said. 'Looks like it's burning. Maybe somebody's set it alight.'

'It could be a trick to draw us away from here,' said Rob. 'I have a feeling that somebody's lying on top of that ridge, watching with field glasses. I'll go out there alone and find out exactly what's happening. You two can arm yourselves, and stand guard here.'

'If that man on the ridge sees you coming, he could finish you off with a rifle bullet,' said Hank.

'I wasn't figuring on letting him see me,' said Rob. 'There's plenty of cover around here to allow a man on foot to circle round and come up to that ridge from the far side, without being seen. So that's what I'll do.'

As he finished speaking, Marian joined them, and saw the smoke still billowing upwards. Rob told her what he was proposing to do.

'Sounds mighty dangerous to me,' said Marian. 'Who knows what's waiting out there for you.'

'That's what I want to find out,' said Rob. 'I aim to sneak up on foot on anybody out there without them seeing me. I'll be back as soon as I can.'

Rob was already wearing his Peacemaker. He went to pick up his Winchester rifle. Then, screened by the house from a possible watcher on top of the ridge, he bent forward and ran to a tree-fringed creek running nearby. He moved quickly along the creek until he could see a route leading from the creek to the far side of the ridge which would be out of view of the possible watcher. He followed this route until he rounded the end of the ridge, where he paused.

Looking along it, he could see, some way off, smoke still rising from the burning brush. Cautiously, he started moving towards this. As he drew closer, he saw a horse standing at the foot of the ridge, well away from the fire, which was now dying down. There was no sign of its rider. He continued a little way past the horse, and then started to climb up the side of the ridge, which rose to meet a narrow, level stretch of ground at the top.

Moving as silently as he could, and keeping a watchful eye above him, he reached a point near the top of the slope. There he lay down, edged upwards, and peered along the narrow top of the ridge. He stiffened as he saw a man lying on his stomach only twenty yards away. The man was looking through field glasses in the direction of the Crazy L ranch house. On the ground by his side lay a rifle.

Silently, Rob eased himself over the top of the slope, rose to his feet, and moved slowly and carefully towards the man lying on the ground and stopped short a few paces away. His six-gun was in his hand. He laid his rifle on the ground.

'Just stay right where you are,' he called out. 'Make a move of any kind, and you get a bullet in the back.'

Sweeney froze, still holding the field glasses up to his eyes. Never before, in his nefarious career, had he found himself at such a disadvantage. Generally, his victim had been assassinated without being aware of his killer's presence. Rob stepped up to him, took his six-gun, and threw this and his rifle aside. He ordered Sweeney to roll over, then sit up facing him. Cursing inwardly, Sweeney recognized Rob from Vickery's description. His plan to draw Rob towards the ridge, to be killed by a rifle bullet, had gone badly wrong.

'I figure Vickery sent you,' said Rob, 'and from the look of you it wouldn't surprise me to hear that you're wanted by the law. What I'm going to do is take you back to the Crazy L ranch house. We'll hold you there, and get a lawman to come and pick you up.'

Rob stepped backwards with the intention of picking up his rifle. As he was bending down to do this, he saw, out of the corner of his eye, the rapid movement of his prisoner's hand towards the Smith and Wesson Pocket .32 revolver concealed in a special pocket on the inside of his vest. With lightning speed, born of long practice, Sweeney pulled out the weapon and swung it round to bear on Rob. But even so, he was a fraction too slow. Before he had triggered his gun, a bullet from Rob's Peacemaker struck him squarely on the forehead. He died instantly, and collapsed on the ground. Conscious of his narrow escape, Rob looked through the dead man's pockets, but found nothing to identify him.

He dragged the body down the slope to the horse, and slung it over the back of the animal. The brush fire had now died out. He collected all the weapons and the field glasses, then led the horse through a gap in the ridge, and back to the ranch house. Marian and the hands, who had been anxiously watching out since Rob's departure, saw him coming. As he walked up to them, they stared at the body on the horse.

'This man was lying in ambush on top of the ridge,' said Rob. 'I got the drop on him, and I was figuring to hold him prisoner here for a lawman to pick up. But he pulled this fancy pocket gun from under his vest, and it was either him or me. He died on the spot. Does any of you know him? Is he from the Circle Dot?'

The two hands walked up and looked at the dead man's face. Both shook their heads.

'Never seen him before,' said Hank.

'My guess is,' said Rob, 'that he's a gunfighter hired by Vickery to do his dirty work. The question is, what do we do with him? Maybe we should just bury him near here, and say nothing about what's just happened.'

'I reckon you're right,' said Luke. 'Let's leave Vickery wondering why his hired killer has disappeared.'

Marian took Rob in to see her father, who was now sitting up in bed. They told him what had happened, and he agreed that the body should be buried, and that the incident should be kept quiet.

'It's pretty clear to us now,' said the rancher, 'that Vickery's set on taking over the Crazy L, whatever it takes. But we still have no definite proof that he's behind what's been happening here.'

'You're right,' said Rob. 'There ain't nothing we can do but carry on as before, and deal with any trouble that comes along.'

A little later, Sweeney was buried inside a small group of trees near the creek.

6

On the Circle Dot, on the morning of the day after Rob's encounter with Sweeney, Vickery was getting concerned over the non-appearance of the man he had hired to kill Rob. Sweeney had left the ranch before daybreak the previous day, after getting as much information as he could about the terrain on the Crazy L, in particular about the ridge where Rob had later found him. He had told Vickery that he expected to be back at the ranch within twenty-four hours.

Aware of Sweeney's record of one hundred per cent success, Vickery was even more puzzled and concerned when the outlaw did not return that day or the day following. Nor was there any news in Brody of any untoward incident on the Crazy L. The only news picked up was that Lee was recovering well from his gunshot wound. It was while

Vickery was in a state of indecision over what his next move should be that Nolan rode up to the ranch house, accompanied by Turner and Haley.

Nolan, a distant relative of Vickery, occasionally used the Circle Dot as a hideout, and he was aware of Vickery's cattle rustling activities, and his intention to take over the Crazy L to provide range for his increasing herd. Nolan was intending to stay a short while at the Circle Dot before embarking on his next criminal operation. Through a contact in Amarillo he had received wind of a valuable shipment by stagecoach, over the route running south from Amarillo, in two weeks time. One of his men, Radford, had quit the gang, and as he had told Vickery, Nolan was looking for a suitable replacement. But this was not essential for the forthcoming robbery.

Inside the ranch house, Nolan told Vickery of the coming operation. Then the rancher told the outlaw that he had, without success, sounded out the stranger Sinclair about joining up with a gang of lawbreakers, not mentioning any names.

'He showed he was mighty handy with a six-gun,' said Vickery, 'which was why I sounded him out for you. But the next I heard, he was working for Lee on the Crazy L. I hired Sweeney to get rid of him, but now Sweeney's just gone and disappeared. I don't know what's happened to him. And Sinclair's still alive.'

'Looks like you need our help to get rid of Sinclair,' said Nolan. 'We've got a bit of time to spare. Tell me all about Sinclair and the Crazy L.'

When Vickery had done this he went on to tell Nolan about his latest thoughts on how to deal with the problem.

'It looks like I'm going to have to kill off everybody at the Crazy L, including Sinclair,' he said. 'I need the extra range; I don't want anybody living nearby to watch what I'm doing; and I want to make the ranch as safe as it can be for folks like you who want to hide out for a spell.'

'I can see the fix you're in,' said Nolan. 'What plan did you have in mind?'

'To kill them all off, and leave them there to be found dead,' said Vickery, 'just wouldn't work. I'd be suspected for sure, and the law would come snooping around. And that I *don't* want. My idea was to get rid of the bodies so that they'd never be found, then to put the story round that Lee had suddenly decided on selling the Crazy L and leaving for California. It so happens he was talking about doing that a few years back. But then he changed his mind. Folks around here will remember that.

'There's a crooked lawyer in Brody who's made out forged bills of sale for me for rustled cattle. If I pay him well enough, he'll forge the documents transferring the Crazy L to me. I'm sure he has samples of Lee's signature in his files.'

'That sounds like a good plan to me,' said Nolan. 'But everybody on the

Crazy L will be keeping a close watch for anybody from the Circle Dot heading in their direction. So what if my men Turner and Haley rode in there, casual like, from the north, and pretended to be trail hands riding back to South Texas after driving a trail herd up to Wyoming. Two men riding in like that would stand a chance of being believed, but any more would cause suspicion. Did anyone from the Crazy L see Turner when he was here before?'

'No,' said Walton the ramrod, who had followed Nolan into the house earlier. 'I can vouch for that. I took him into Brody, but we met nobody from the Crazy L.'

'Good,' said Nolan. 'What I'll do then is to get Turner and Haley to ride up to the Crazy L ranch house. They'll be dressed like trail hands and they won't be wearing gunbelts. But each of them will carry a six-gun tucked into the top of his pants, underneath his vest. Both are real handy with a pistol, and if they can put Sinclair and the others off their guard, the folks on the Crazy L won't stand a chance. They'll tend to Sinclair first, then deal with the others. As for getting rid of the bodies, what did you have in mind?'

'There's a cave in a hillside on my range,' said Vickery. 'There's a deep pit in the floor of the cave, so deep we've never been able to measure it. I was aiming to drop the bodies down there, where they'd never be found. I'll ride into Brody right now and get those documents from the lawyer. Then maybe Haley and Turner could pay that visit to the Crazy L tomorrow.'

'All right,' said Nolan. 'I'll talk with them and tell them exactly what we want them to do.'

*   *   *

On the following day on the Crazy L, early in the afternoon, Luke was on watch. Looking to the north, he first spotted the two riders when they were some distance away. He called Rob and Hank, who joined him. Marian and her father, who was now sitting up in an armchair for part of the time, were in his bedroom. Quickly, Rob checked that there were no further riders approaching from other directions. Then he stood with Hank and Luke. Each of them was carrying a six-gun, and rifles were standing in the nearby walkway between the house and the bunkhouse. Additionally, hidden just behind Rob, standing against the end of a water trough, was a double-barrelled shotgun, a weapon extolled by Rob's mentor, Will Cartwright, the old bounty hunter, as a fearsome weapon ideal for use in certain circumstances.

'Be ready for trouble, in case these two start anything,' said Rob. 'And let me do the talking.'

As the two riders cantered towards them, Marian came out of the house and joined the others. As Haley and Turner drew close, Marian and the two hands told Rob that the riders were strangers to them. And so far as they could all see, the two men were not wearing handguns.

The riders stopped in front of Rob and the others, pleased to see that all their intended victims, except for the injured Lee, were standing in front of them. Looking up at them, Rob had a vague feeling that somewhere he had seen the two men before. But he could not recollect when and where. Turner, who had the ability to hide his true character behind a façade of friendliness and bonhomie, smiled expansively down at them and spoke.

'Howdy folks,' he said. 'My partner and me, we gone and got ourselves lost. We helped drive a trail herd up to Wyoming a while back, and now we're riding back to San Antonio. We was figuring to call in at Brody. Are we anywhere near?'

'You've come a mite too far,' said Rob, closely watching the two. 'Brody's about seven miles northwest of here.'

'Darn it,' said Turner. 'We'll have to

ride back there. We need some supplies. But before we ride there, we'd be obliged if our mounts could take a drink from the water trough there.'

'Sure,' said Rob, almost convinced that these two men presented no danger.

Haley and Turner dismounted in unison and each stood for a moment facing the side of his horse. Their right hands, out of view of Rob and his companions, reached for the six-guns concealed under their vests. As they were dismounting, Rob took another close look at them, and suddenly realized that he was almost certainly looking at Turner and Haley, members of the Nolan gang, portrayed on the wanted posters in his possession. Quickly, he reached down behind him, took hold of the shotgun, and cocked the hammers.

The two outlaws moved along the sides of their horses, holding their six-guns out of sight behind them. Their intention was to step out in front of their mounts and gun down Rob and his companions before they realized the danger they were in. Then they would dispose of the wounded Lee, put the bodies on a buckboard, and take them to the Cave mentioned by Vickery.

But when they stepped out in front of their horses, and were bringing their guns round to bear on their targets, they were suddenly confronted by Rob holding a cocked shotgun pointing at them. They froze, knowing full well the lethal effect of a load of buckshot propelled from a shotgun at close range.

'You can drop the guns,' said Rob, and the two men complied. Then, with the help of Hank and Luke, Rob took the two prisoners into the barn. They were tied securely hand and foot, and were left lying on the floor, while Rob and the others went outside to discuss the situation. Marian joined them. But first, Rob got the wanted posters for Turner and Haley from his room, and showed them to the others. The likeness, in each case, was unmistakable. A knife scar on Haley's face, mentioned in the poster, confirmed his identity beyond doubt.

'That was a close call we just had,' said Rob. 'I reckon Vickery brought Nolan in to help get rid of us, and Nolan sent Haley and Turner to do the job. At last we can bring the law in. Haley and Turner are both wanted men. Our problem is that we've got to hang on to the prisoners till the law gets here. And that could take a little while. What I'll do is send a message to Marshal Kennedy in Amarillo. He knows me and he knows what I'm doing here. I know that the stagecoach route running south from Amarillo is a little way east of here. If we can get a message in a sealed envelope marked private and urgent to the nearest swing station, the driver of the first north-bound coach would make sure it got to Marshal Kennedy with nobody but us knowing the contents.'

'The nearest swing station is about twelve miles north-east of here,' said

Hank. 'You'd better let me take the message. I know the stock tender in charge of the station. He's a friend of mine. I can reach the station without going anywhere near the Circle Dot.'

'All right,' said Rob. 'I'll write the message now. I expect we've got a little time before Vickery and Nolan realize their plan has failed. For the time being, Luke, you'd better stand guard over the two prisoners in the barn. Take the shotgun with you. I'm going to write that message. Meantime, Hank, you watch out for any riders heading this way.'

Rob went into the house with Marian, and she handed him a sheet of paper and a stout envelope. Then she went to tell her father what had happened. Rob sat down and wrote the message. In it he told Kennedy that he was holding Haley and Turner prisoner on the Crazy L. He said that he suspected that Nolan himself was in league with Vickery, the owner of the adjacent Circle Dot, and that they would be making an attempt to free the prisoners. He asked the marshal to send help as soon as possible to pick up Haley and Turner and deal with Nolan and Vickery, who were threatening the lives of everyone on the Crazy L. He put the message in the envelope, which he sealed, then addressed it to US MARSHAL KENNEDY, AMARILLO. He marked the envelope URGENT AND PRIVATE.

He took the letter to Hank, who had saddled up and was waiting to leave. Hank told him that he would probably reach the swing station about half an hour before a northbound stage was due to call there.

'Good,' said Rob. 'Don't say anything about what's in the letter, but make sure the driver's told how urgent it is.'

Five minutes later Hank departed and Rob went to see Lee. Marian was with her father. Rob told the rancher what the message contained, and said that Hank was now carrying it to the swing station.

Lee, lying in bed, and still very weak, was clearly worried.

'I sure hope Hank gets back safe,' he said. 'And can the posse get here in time, considering the number of men we're facing?'

'It ain't going to be easy,' said Rob, 'but I reckon we can do it if we plan things right. Now I'd best go outside and keep watch for a while.'

He left the house, and walked over to the barn. The two prisoners looked at Rob as he came in. They did not speak. Luke was sitting on a box a few yards from them, with the shotgun lying across his thighs.

'I'll be outside if you want me, Luke,' said Rob.

He checked that there were no riders in sight, then went to stand outside the house, his mind searching for an answer to the problems facing them. A few minutes later Marian came out to join him. He could see that she was deeply troubled.

'How's it all going to end, Rob?' she

asked. 'Are we all going to die?'

'I've just had an idea,' said Rob, 'that should keep us alive until the posse turns up. I reckon Hank stands a good chance of getting back here safe, before the real trouble starts. He's going to borrow a fresh horse at the swing station for the ride back here. I'm guessing it'll be a while before Vickery and Nolan realize that their plan has failed.

'What we need to do now, Marian, is bring the two prisoners into the house. That's the best place to guard them. Where could we put them?'

'There's that storeroom off the living room,' said Marian. 'It has a door, but no window. They could stay in there.'

'Right,' said Rob. 'We'll move them in there right now.'

The prisoners were brought to the storeroom. The ropes binding their hands and feet were double-checked and they were left lying on the floor. It was growing dark outside.

'It's not all that far to the Circle Dot

ranch house,' said Rob to Marian and Luke. 'I'm going to take a message there. I figure to deliver it without being seen. Then I'll come straight back here.'

He got a sheet of paper from Marian, plus a small canvas bag and some string. Luke went outside and found him a piece of rock which fitted nicely into the palm of his hand. He wrote the message down on the paper and showed it to Marian and Luke, then her father. He put the message in the bag and tied this to the piece of rock.

'I'll leave now,' he said. 'You keep guard, Luke, and remember, when Hank gets near the house he'll shout the password 'crazy'. I'll do the same.'

As Rob rode off into the gathering darkness, Marian prayed for his safe return.

Approaching the Circle Dot buildings, Rob could see lights in the house and the cookshack. He stopped well short of the house and picketed his horse. Carefully, he approached the buildings on foot. There was no sign of men outside them. He guessed that supper was in progress in the cookshack and the ranch house.

He halted a few feet from a large window in the house. A curtain was drawn across it inside. He grasped the piece of rock firmly in his right hand and threw it at the centre of one of the large panes of glass. The glass shattered and the rock, with the canvas bag attached, bellied out the curtain and fell to the floor inside. Immediately, Rob turned and raced back to his horse, and before the alarm could be raised he was well away from the buildings, heading for the Crazy L. On arrival there he called out the password and was relieved to find that Hank had arrived earlier. Hank told him that the stagecoach had arrived on schedule at the swing station, and that Marshal Kennedy should receive the message tomorrow evening.

'Good,' said Rob. 'Tonight, we'll station a guard as usual. And the guard will make a regular check on the prisoners. And remember, I told Kennedy in the message that if the posse turned up here in the dark, they should use the password 'crazy', just like Hank and I did.'

7

In one corner of the large living room in the Circle Dot ranch house, Vickery, Walton and Nolan were seated at a table taking supper and awaiting expectantly the return of Turner and Haley. Their conversation had ceased for the moment, and they were all busy eating when suddenly the silence was shattered by the sound of breaking glass, and a piece of rock, with a small bag tied to it, landed on the floor near the table. The three men jumped up, stared down at the missile, then picked up their six-guns from a nearby table and ran out of the house. But there was no sign of the person responsible for the incident.

They went back indoors. Vickery picked up the piece of rock and detached the bag. From inside it he took the sheet of paper and read the message on it, scrawled in large capital letters. The message was addressed to Vickery and Nolan. It read:

Holding Nolan gang members Turner and Haley prisoner on Crazy L. Try to rescue them or attack anybody on the ranch and the prisoners will be shot dead. Sinclair.

Vickery read the brief message. Shocked, he passed it to Nolan, who read it, then handed it to Walton. All three quickly realized the serious implications raised by the message.

'This is real bad news,' said Nolan. 'Sinclair knows, or guesses, that I'm here on the Circle Dot. He knows who Haley and Turner are. He's bound to contact the law to ask them to pick up his prisoners and look into what's been happening on the Crazy L lately. But it's going to be a while before the law turns up here. At least a day and a half, I reckon.

'You've got plenty of men, Vickery. How about us making an all-out attack tonight on the Crazy L to finish off Sinclair and the others? If Haley and Turner get killed, that's too bad. Whatever happens, we could make it look like those two killed Sinclair and the others, then rode off.'

'I don't like the sound of that,' said Vickery. 'Likely I'd lose some of my men. There's no real proof that I had anything to do with what's been happening on the Crazy L. Maybe we should just let the law take Turner and Haley in. They would naturally be suspected of shooting Lee. And like I said, there's no real evidence against *me*.'

Some time later they were still discussing the situation, with no signs of them reaching an agreement, when they heard a loud knocking on the door of the house. Walton went to see who was there. He returned shortly after with a man called Dixon, the leader of a criminal gang of three who had used the Circle Dot as a hideout from time to time.

Vickery introduced him to Nolan, whom he had not met before. Then

Dixon told them he couldn't stay long, but had just called in passing to hand over some important information to Vickery.

'A few hours ago,' he told them, 'me and my gang held up a stagecoach. It was heading north for Amarillo. The driver had no sense at all. Went for a shotgun on the seat beside him. I had to shoot him down off his box. The fool died on the spot. Anyhow, we made a pretty good haul from the passengers. When I checked the driver to see if he had any cash on him, I found an envelope addressed to the US marshal in Amarillo.'

He took an envelope from his pocket.

'I was curious about what was in it,' he went on, 'so I took it with me when we left the stagecoach and headed for a hideout on the border with New Mexico Territory. A mile after we'd left the coach I took a look at the message inside. Could see you'd be mighty interested in what was in it. I wasn't far from the Circle Dot ranch house, so the others rode on to the hideout, while I branched off and came here. I aim to follow them.'

He handed the envelope to Vickery, who took out the message and read it. As he passed it over for Nolan and Walton to read, the relief on his face was evident.

'You done us a real good turn, Dixon,' he said. 'There's free board and lodging for you and your men any time you want to stay here.'

'I'll take you up on that,' said Dixon. 'But right now I'm heading off to join up with my men.'

'That was a real stroke of luck,' said Vickery, when Dixon had left. 'Now that we've got a password there's nothing to stop us from raiding the Crazy L to capture Sinclair and the others, and free Turner and Haley.'

'You're right,' said Nolan. 'Sinclair would expect the posse to arrive not by tomorrow night, but maybe by the night after. So that's when we should make our move. Having the password will help us get right up to them, but to get the most advantage out of that we need to send two men ahead who aren't known to anybody on the Crazy L.'

He explained his plan to the others.

'That's a good idea,' said Vickery. 'As for the two strangers we need, Ford and Arnold rode in earlier today, figuring to hide out here from the law for a few days. Maybe they'll help us out. I'll talk with them in the morning. And like I suggested before, we'll take all the prisoners to that cave I mentioned and drop them into the pit. I've got the forged papers from the lawyer in town transferring the Crazy L to me. And the story in town is that Lee's recovered far enough so that the doctor ain't going to visit him for another week. So it seems like he *could* set out for California if he had a mind.'

The following morning Vickery approached Ford and Arnold, who agreed to help him in the forthcoming raid.

★　★　★

On the Crazy L on the morning following the capture of Haley and Turner, there was relief that there had been no attack during the night. Unable to assess what the reaction of Vickery and Nolan would be to Rob's message, they remained constantly watchful during that day, the night that followed, and the day after that. As darkness was falling, Rob took a few minutes off watch to speak to the others, including Lee, who were taking supper in the house. He told them there was a good chance that the posse would turn up during the night and whoever was on guard would have to listen out for the password and alert the others if they heard it. Then he returned to his post.

Hank, who relieved Rob at midnight, heard the faint voice calling out of the darkness around two in the morning. He could clearly here the word 'crazy' repeated several times. He alerted Luke and Rob who joined him a minute later. The password was still being called out, gradually getting louder, until they could see the shapes of two horses and riders looming out of the darkness. The two mounts came to a stop.

'Leave your horses there and walk in and show yourselves,' Rob called out. 'And I'm warning you, I've got a double-barrelled shotgun pointing straight at you.'

Ford and Arnold walked up with their hands raised. They stopped in front of Rob and the others. Luke picked up a lantern, lit it, and they all looked closely at the faces of the two men who had just rode in. They were complete strangers. The light revealed that each of them was wearing the badge of the Texas Rangers. The badges had, in fact, been provided by Nolan, who had taken them from two Texas Rangers the gang had ambushed and killed some time ago.

As Luke lowered the lamp Ford spoke. 'Marshal Kennedy asked the Rangers to carry out this operation,' he said. 'I'm Ranger Benson. This is Ranger Brennan with me. I'm in charge of the posse. There's ten others waiting out there. They'll come in either when I call them or when they hear gunfire. But first, tell me what the present situation is here.'

'I'm Sinclair,' said Rob. 'Let's go inside.'

They all entered the house, with Rob bringing up the rear. Marian and her father were already there, having been alerted by Rob earlier. Rob introduced them and the two hands to the two men who had just arrived. There was nothing in their appearance to indicate they were anthing other than two of the lawmen they were expecting.

Hank and Luke returned their six-guns to their holsters and Rob released the hammers on the shotgun and laid it on a nearby table. Then he told the two bogus rangers that since he had sent the message to the US marshal, there had been no further attack on the Crazy L.

'You've got the two prisoners here in the house?' asked Ford.

Rob pointed to the door of the storeroom. 'In there,' he said.

He walked towards the door, with Ford following him. As he reached it Ford suddenly drew his six-gun and pistol-whipped Rob on the side of his head. As Rob collapsed on the floor, temporarily stunned, Marian screamed. Simultaneously Arnold, standing against the table, picked up the shotgun. He pulled back the two hammers, and pointed it at Marian and her father and the two hands before Hank and Luke, slow to react, could draw their weapons. Staring into the barrels of the shotgun, they all froze.

Ford turned to check that his partner had the situation under control. He took Rob's Peacemaker, then opened the storeroom door and went inside. Shortly after, he came out with Turner and Haley, both moving stiffly after the long period of inaction. He had briefly explained to them that he and his partner had been sent by Vickery and Nolan. The two men glared angrily at

Rob and the others, still smarting from the way they had been captured and held prisoner. Rob stirred, then tried to sit up. Marian ran to help him as he climbed groggily to his feet. He stood looking at the four outlaws.

All five prisoners' hands were tied and they were seated on the floor with their backs to the wall. Arnold stood guard over them, still holding the shotgun, while Ford went outside to call in Vickery, Nolan and the three Circle Dot hands waiting in the darkness. When they arrived, Ford told them of the successful outcome of the operation and led Vickery and Nolan into the house. The others stayed outside.

In the living room Vickery looked down on Rob and the others with grim satisfaction. Then, leaving Arnold to guard the prisoners, he led the others outside to discuss the next move.

'We'll stick to my original plan,' he said. 'We'll divide our party. Some of us will lay all five prisoners on the Crazy L buckboard and take them to the cave. Once there, they'll be dropped in the pit and the buckboard will be returned to the Crazy L. The rest of us will go through the house and bunkhouse and sort out all the personal belongings they'd be likely to take if they actually *were* heading for California, and travelling light. These will be taken back to the Circle Dot on the buckboard we brought with us. The question is, who's going to take the prisoners to the cave?'

'That's something Haley and me would really like to do,' said Turner, and Haley nodded assent.

Vickery looked at Nolan, who nodded his head.

'All right,' said Vickery, 'but take Ford and Arnold with you. We can't afford to take the slightest chance of any of them getting away.'

The prisoners' feet were untied and they were led to the buckboard which was standing near the house. Rob, certain that the intention of Vickery and Nolan was to murder all their prisoners, was determined to seize the slightest chance of turning the tables on their captors. As he was standing by the buckboard he overheard Turner refer to the two bogus rangers as Ford and Arnold. But the names meant nothing to him. He was the first to climb on the buckboard and he purposely lay on his back against the right-hand side, with his head behind the driver's seat. Marian followed him, then the others. And once again their feet were tied.

When the buckboard set off briskly towards the cave shortly after, Ford was driving it, with Arnold sitting by his side. Their horses were tied on behind. Turner and Haley led the way on their mounts. The night was dark. Marian's father, although still weak, was bearing up well. Rob's head was aching, but was quite clear. They had no idea where the buckboard was taking them.

On the previous day, Rob had been discussing with Luke some repairs which were required on the buckboard on which they were now lying. One of the panels on the right-hand side of the vehicle had been broken and had fallen away. It needed replacement. In addition, the metal tyre on the rear right-hand wheel was quite thin and had shifted so that it was projecting slightly from the edge of the rim towards the side of the buckboard. The two men had decided to have it repaired by the blacksmith in Brody when the opportunity arose.

Slowly, Rob twisted round a little so that his back was to the hole in the side of the vehicle. Marian was lying close beside him and he whispered into her ear that he was going to try and free his hands. Fearful of what lay ahead, she nodded to him, wondering if there could possibly be the slightest glimmer of hope in what seemed to be a dire situation. She relayed Rob's whispered message to her father who was lying by her side. It was then passed to Luke and Hank.

Pushing his hands through the gap, Rob felt with his fingers for the wheel, which was quite close to the side of the buckboard. He could feel it rotating. He moved his hands and could feel with his fingers the sharp moving edge of the protruding metal tyre. The problem facing him was that of positioning his hands in exactly the right place behind him so that the edge of the rotating tyre would cut through the rope joining his wrists together. He knew it was likely to be a long and difficult process. He wondered how long their journey on the buckboard was to be.

With some difficulty he managed to get his hands in the right position and could feel that the edge of the tyre was rubbing against the rope. But a few minutes later a rut in the ground caused a jolt which temporarily destroyed the alignment and Rob received a shallow cut on the side of his hand. He repositioned his hands, but the same thing happened again and continued to do so, from time to time, as the journey progressed.

After a while, Rob's arms began to ache and he found it more and more difficult to hold the rope firmly against the edge of the tyre. He fancied that maybe one or more of the strands on the rope had parted but he could not be sure. Losing all count of time, and ignoring the pain from the numerous cuts on his hands and wrists, he concentrated on maintaining contact between the rope and the tyre. From time to time, Arnold twisted on his seat and looked down on the prisoners. But in the darkness there was no indication of Rob's attempt to free himself.

Then, as the buckboard continued on its way, Rob noticed two things. The sky was lightening in the east. And looking under the seat he saw, directly ahead of them, the dim outline of a hill. Fearful that they may be nearing the end of their journey, he redoubled his efforts. When they were about thirty yards from the foot of the hill the last strand in the rope suddenly parted, just as Turner and Haley were dismounting outside the cave. A moment later they entered it to illuminate it with an oil lamp that Haley had brought with him.

Rob felt the buckboard slowing down. It was clear that there was no time for him to attempt to untie the rope around his ankles. His hands now free, he twisted round, pulled himself forward, and reached up with his right hand to pull out the six-gun from Arnold's holster. Arnold felt the weapon being withdrawn and he called out to his partner. At the same time he pulled out Rob's six-gun, which he had decided to keep, from underneath his belt. Both the outlaws twisted round, each with a gun in his hand. Rob knew that only a supreme effort on his part could save the lives of himself and his helpless companions.

With deadly accuracy, he shot Arnold through the head just before the outlaw was ready to trigger his gun. Rob's six-gun swung rapidly in a short arc and Ford was also hit in the head. But Rob was not unscathed. Ford had fired simultaneously, though without Rob's precision, and his bullet had gouged the flesh near the top of Rob's left arm. Both outlaws were instantly dead. Ford fell sideways off the buckboard. Arnold fell sideways along the seat and Rob was able to pluck the knife from his belt. Quickly, he slashed through the ropes binding his ankles. He freed Luke's hands, then looked towards the hill in the growing light. He could see two horses standing near what looked like the entrance to a cave.

'Free everybody, Luke,' he said, urgently. 'The two men I just shot are dead. From what I heard, Haley and Turner were leading them somewhere. Those must be their horses. Likely they've gone into that cave. I'm going after them now. Make everybody here stay right where they are.'

Quickly, he checked the gun he was carrying. Only three cartridges remained. He jumped down from the buckboard, knowing that the men in the cave would probably have heard the gunfire and would be appearing at any moment. With the gun in his hand he ran towards the hill, aiming for a point to the right of the cave entrance where a large boulder standing near the foot of the slope would give him some cover. He had almost reached it when Turner and Haley ran out of the cave and spotted him. But he disappeared behind the boulder before they could fire. He stayed there out of sight, knowing that he must use his remaining bullets effectively to put the two outlaws out of action. Turner and Haley stood facing the boulder, waiting for Rob to show himself.

The impasse was resolved by a burst of fire from the buckboard. Luke had freed Hank, then had seen Rob take cover behind the boulder. He picked up Rob's Peacemaker, which had fallen from Arnold's hand, and fired four hasty shots over the end of the buckboard in the general direction of Turner and Haley. The shots did no damage but they pro-duced the distraction which was all that

Rob needed. The outlaws looked towards the buckboard. Rob stepped out from behind the boulder. As Turner and Haley turned back to face it again he shot them both, in rapid succession, in the heart, before they were ready to fire. He walked up to the bodies lying on the ground and confirmed that both men were dead. He took their guns.

Looking towards the buckboard he could see Hank and Luke watching him. He waved to them, then went into the cave, which was still illuminated by an oil lamp. He came out shortly after and ran to the buckboard where the four freed prisoners were climbing down to the ground.

'Those shots you fired,' he said, 'were just what I needed to help me get the better of Turner and Haley. They're both dead. Inside that cave is a deep pit. I reckon the plan was that we should all be dropped in it. It'll be a while before Vickery and Nolan know we've escaped. I reckon we should head for Brody. We'll be safe there. And we can send another message to Marshal Kennedy. It's clear that somehow Vickery got hold of the first one I sent.'

'I think you're right,' said Lee. 'And we don't want to waste no time. I can ride a horse there if we take it easy.'

Marian noticed the blood coming from Rob's wound, and insisted on looking at it. It was not deep. Quickly she padded and bound it with two bandannas. Then they took the four bodies into the cave and left them lying there. They departed for Brody shortly after. Four of them were riding the dead men's horses. Rob was riding one horse from the buckboard bareback, and leading the other.

8

Rob and his companions reached Brody two hours before noon. They rode up to the livery stable and dismounted. They had seen no other riders during their journey. They went into the stable. Randle, surprised to see everyone from the Crazy L in town at one time, greeted them. They told the liveryman of recent developments.

Randle was aghast. 'I never figured Vickery would go that far,' he said. 'What are you aiming to do now?'

'We're staying in town till it's safe to go back to the ranch,' said Rob. 'Vickery and Nolan would never try to kill us here. As soon as they find the four bodies in the cave they'll know that the game is up. The first thing we have to do now is get a message to the US marshal in Amarillo. What would be the quickest way to do that?'

'Take the message to the nearest telegraph office at Black Creek, twenty miles north of here,' said Randle. 'Wait while it's being transmitted then stay for the reply.'

'I'll take the message,' said Luke, and Rob looked at the rancher, who nodded his head.

'All right,' said Rob, and asked the liveryman for pen and paper.

'Better have some food and drink while I'm writing this message, Luke,' he said.

'I'll saddle up the best horse I have,' said Randle.

While Rob was writing the telegraph message Marian and her father went to the doctor's house, and told him the news. Astonished at the turn of events, he looked at Lee's wound.

'You're lucky,' he said. 'It hasn't opened up. Looks quite healthy. But you'd better rest for a while. Stay here in my spare room for the time being.'

'I'll take you up on that,' said Lee. 'I've got to say I'm plumb tuckered out.'

'Rob will be here to see you shortly,

Doctor,' said Marian. 'He's writing that message to the US marshal. He was shot in the arm. But I think it's only a flesh wound.'

Rob came in a few minutes later. He was carrying the message. He showed it to the rancher, after which it was read by Marian and Doc Fender. The message went:

Nolan gang members Turner and Haley dead. Two criminals Ford and Arnold also dead. All four killed while attempting murder of self and four others on the Crazy L ranch near Brody, Texas, north of Fort Worth. Nolan in cahoots with Vickery owner of Circle Dot ranch near Brody. Vickery suspected of hiding criminals. Myself and everybody from Crazy L now sheltering in Brody. There's a chance you can capture Nolan and Vickery and others if you move fast. Luke Warner of Crazy L is waiting in Black Creek for reply to this message. Rob Sinclair.

'My guess is,' said Rob, 'that as soon as those four are found dead in the cave, Nolan and Vickery will realize that the game is up, and they'll be aiming to ride off before the law gets here. So there is a chance the posse will turn up too late to capture them here.'

He left and went back to the stable, where Luke had just turned up. Rob showed him the message and Luke rode off with it a few minutes later. Rob returned to the doctor's house and Fender examined the wound.

'Nothing serious,' he said. 'I'll clean it up and bandage it for you. And I'll tend to those cuts on your hands and wrists.'

When this had been done Rob, with Marian and her father, joined Hank and they all took a meal at the hotel. Then Lee returned to the doctor's house. The others took rooms at the hotel where they decided to take some much needed rest while waiting for Luke's return.

* * *

When Luke reached Black Creek, he went straight to the telegraph office and watched while the message was transmitted. Then he told the operator that he was going to take some rest at the hotel. He asked him to make sure he got the reply as soon as it came through.

Luke was given the reply, addressed to him, two hours later. It read:

Ranger Captain Denny in Fort Worth has authorized use of posse of Texas Rangers on this operation. Posse at present returning to Fort Worth. Due to call at Black Creek later today. Ranger Colby in charge. Show him this message which he will take as an order to accompany you immediately to Brody and deal with the situation. Kennedy US Marshal Amarillo.

Ninety minutes later Luke was sitting in a chair by the window in his hotel room when he saw the posse of twelve Texas Rangers ride into town. He left the hotel and walked over to the saloon, outside which the men had just finished dismounting.

'Ranger Colby?' he asked.

One of the men turned to face Luke. 'That's me,' he said. He was a man in his forties, tough and weather beaten, with a look of authority about him. Without comment, Luke handed him a copy of Rob's message and the reply. Colby studied both of them closely. Then he turned to the rangers.

'You've got one hour exactly,' he said, 'to see to the horses and get yourselves some food and drink. Then we ride to Brody.'

He turned to Luke, who gave him a quick account of events leading up to the call to the US marshal for help.

'I'll be riding to Brody with you,' he said.

They arrived in Brody in the evening and Luke took Colby to see Rob and Hank at the hotel. Marian was with her father at the doctor's house.

'It sure surprises me,' said Rob, 'to see a posse here so quick. This gives us a chance of catching Nolan, as well as Vickery and the other criminals at the Circle Dot. With the nearest ranger station a day and a half's ride away, they'd never expect you to be here so soon.'

'It's pure chance,' said Colby, 'that we had just finished an operation north of here and were riding back to head-quarters. It looks like we should raid the Circle Dot tonight?'

'I reckon so,' said Rob. 'We've had no strangers in town all day, nor anybody from the Circle Dot. So nobody at the ranch knows you're here. We should be able to surprise them if they're still there. I'd like to go along with you. Hank and Luke as well.'

'All right,' said Colby. 'We'll aim to get there just after midnight.'

★　★　★

When Vickery and Nolan arrived back at the Circle Dot after the capture of Rob and the others at the Crazy L they expected Turner and Haley, with Ford and Arnold, to join them there by noon. When this passed, with no sign of the four men, they waited a further hour, then Vickery and Nolan, with two Circle Dot hands, rode to the cave. Inside it, they viewed the four bodies with consternation.

Nolan cursed, devastated at the loss of his two remaining men. 'This means,' he said, 'that Sinclair and the others have escaped. My guess is they're in Brody. We can't touch them there. And by now they've got word to the law about what's been going on here. That means that in less than a couple of days there could be a posse turning up here.'

Vickery was equally shocked. 'We'll have to leave the Circle Dot,' he said. 'Me and the hands will head for the Indian Territory at daybreak. How about you?'

Nolan glanced at the two hands who

had come with them. They were both out of earshot.

'I've got to look for men to build up the gang again,' he said. 'There's a couple of men I know in New Mexico Territory who might be interested. I'm going to ride there. And maybe I can persuade Radford to join up with me again. I'll leave just after dark. And one thing's sure. Sinclair is responsible for killing two of my men. I'll be back to make him pay for what he's done.'

'I'm glad to hear that,' said Vickery. 'What are we going to do with those four bodies?'

'Leave them be,' said Nolan, and he and the others rode off towards the Circle Dot ranch house.

9

The posse arrived in the vicinity of the Circle Dot Ranch buildings half an hour after midnight. Vickery's orders to his men the previous evening had been that during the evening they should pack up all personal belongings which could be carried on horseback. They would then get some sleep and the ranch would be vacated at daybreak. Luther and Murdoch, two outlaws who were staying at the ranch, elected to accompany Vickery and the others to the Indian Territory.

Looking towards the buildings, the posse could see no lights showing from them.

'Maybe they've all left,' said Colby to Rob, 'maybe they're asleep, with guards stationed outside the buildings. We'll soon find out. I have two men with me who are expert at sneaking up on somebody in the dark. They move like shadows. I'll send them in there to report on the situation.'

He walked over and spoke to two of the rangers, who took with them a length of rope and melted into the darkness.

Just over half an hour elapsed before one of the rangers returned, to report that he and his partner had surprised and overcome two guards, who were standing outside the house. They had been knocked unconscious and bound and gagged before they came to. All the signs were that the house and the bunkhouse were occupied. In neither building was the door secured.

The horses ridden by the posse were picketed. The men moved up to the buildings and located some oil lamps in the cookshack and the barn. They lit these. Then Colby split the posse in two. One part silently entered the bunkhouse. The other, including Rob and Colby, moved cautiously into the house. The attack, entirely unexpected by the occupants of both buildings, was a complete success. Not a shot was fired. In the bedrooms in the house, Vickery and Walton were captured, as well as Murdoch and Luther. In the bunkhouse, thirteen hands were taken, including the cook. All the prisoners were escorted to the barn, where they were bound hand and foot, with two rangers guarding them.

In the house, Colby told Rob that he had recognized two of the prisoners as Luther and Murdoch, both wanted for robbery and murder in South Texas.

'All in all,' he said, 'I'd call this a mighty successful operation. From what you tell us, there's also the ones you left lying dead in the cave. Two men from the Nolan gang and Ford and Arnold, who are outlaws we've been after for a long time. But I guess you're pretty disappointed that Nolan himself ain't here, considering what the gang did to your folks.'

'I sure am,' said Rob. 'It's clear he left sometime before we got here. Maybe we can get some information from the prisoners about where he was going when he left here.'

'It's worth trying,' said Colby. 'Nolan's been on the loose far too long.'

'What are you going to do with the prisoners?' asked Rob.

I'll send for a couple of jail wagons to come here and pick them up,' said Colby. 'It's up to Captain Denny, but I reckon the wagons will take them to Black Creek. We'll get a judge to come there to try them. And I guess you'll be the chief witness at the trial.'

'When will the jail wagons get here?' asked Rob.

'Could take up to a week,' Colby replied. 'We'll keep the prisoners here till then, with a few rangers to guard them.'

At daybreak Rob asked Hank and Luke to return to Brody to let Marian and her father know what had happened. He said that he and Colby were riding to the cave where the four bodies had been left. Then he would join them in Brody and they could all return to the Crazy L.

When Rob and Colby reached the cave they found the four bodies still lying on the floor. Colby took a close look at all of them.

'I can confirm,' he said, 'that Ford and Arnold are there, as well as Haley and Turner.'

'I'm riding to Brody now,' said Rob, 'to pick up the others and go out to the Crazy L with them. That's where I'll be if you want me for anything. If you like, I'll ask the undertaker in Brody to come and collect these bodies.'

Colby agreed and they parted company. When Rob reached Brody he talked with the undertaker, then went to see Marian and her father at the doctor's house. Doc Fender was with them. Rob told them of Colby's plan for dealing with the prisoners. Then he spoke to Lee.

'Two of the Nolan gang are accounted for,' he said, 'but I still have to catch up with Nolan and Radford, without any notion right now of where they might be. But for the time being I'll have to stay on around here till the trial's over. If you like, I can carry on helping out at the ranch while you're getting fit again.'

'I'd sure appreciate that,' said the rancher. 'And Marian and me, we want to thank you for helping us out. But for you, I reckon we'd both be dead now. The doc here reckons I should be back to normal in two or three weeks.'

They all took a meal at the hotel, then rode back to the ranch to join Hank and Luke who had left town before them and were already busy at work.

As the days passed while Rob was waiting for the trial to take place, the friendship between him and Marian developed into something which, on Rob's part, was much deeper. She was a lively, attractive young woman with a strong character, devoted to her father. She and Rob had ridden into Brody together one day, and on the way back to the ranch he stopped and spoke to her.

'You know, Marian,' he said, 'that I've *got* to go after Nolan and Radford. If I can, I'm going to hand them over to the law. When that's done I was hoping that maybe we could start a life together. According to Ranger Colby, I've got some reward money coming for those men in the cave. I have a hankering to start ranching, maybe in a small way at first. And my sister in Cheyenne could join us if she wanted. How does the idea strike you? Maybe you'd like some time to think it over?'

She smiled at him. 'No need for that, Rob,' she said. 'I've known for a while that you're the only man for me. I understand why you have to go after those two outlaws. I'm praying you won't get hurt and that it won't take long. When the job's done I'll be here waiting for you. And about your sister. If she decides to join us, I'd be real glad of some female company. One thing, though. I wouldn't want to be living too far away from my father.'

'I already figured that,' said Rob. 'It

goes without saying that we'll choose a place that suits us both.'

They kissed and continued on their way. When they reached the ranch house Rob went to see Lee, who was resting in the living room. He told him of his hope that he and Marian could marry and run a ranch as soon as he had dealt with Nolan and Radford.

'I ain't blind,' said the rancher. 'I could see the way things were going. Marian's a good girl, and I'm sure going to miss her. But she has a right to live her own life. I'm mighty glad to hear that your gunfighting days will be over when Nolan and Radford have been caught. I had the thought that you would want to carry on as a lawman, or maybe a bounty hunter.'

'I learnt how to handle a gun well for only one reason,' said Rob, 'and that was to make sure the outlaws who killed my parents were made to pay for what they did. I get no pleasure out of shooting a man down.'

Two days later Ranger Colby called

at the Crazy L to ask Rob to ride with him to Black Creek, where the trial was to be held the following day. He told Rob that all the prisoners had been questioned about where Nolan was going when he left the Circle Dot. The interrogations had been in vain.

'But,' said Colby, 'Marshal Kennedy's going to let you know at the ranch here if he gets any report of Nolan or Radford being sighted.'

'I appreciate that,' said Rob, 'because right now I don't have the slightest notion of where to start looking.'

At the trial the following day, it emerged that some rustled cattle had been found on the Circle Dot. They had been taken from a small ranch a hundred miles to the north in an operation during which the rancher had been badly wounded and his two hands killed. After Rob and others had given their testimonies the judge announced the sentences, based on the evidence put before the court.

Vickery and his ramrod, and two of

his hands, were sentenced to death by hanging. The same sentence was imposed in the cases of Luther and Murdoch. The remaining Circle Dot hands received custodial sentences of varying lengths.

After the trial, Colby passed on to Rob an invitation from Ranger Captain Denny to join the Texas Rangers at Fort Worth. Rob declined.

'I aim to find Nolan and Radford,' he said. 'Then I plan to marry and settle down.'

Rob returned to the Crazy L to help out with the work and await any news from Marshal Kennedy.

On the Circle Dot, steps had been initiated by the Texas Rangers for the stolen cattle to be returned to their rightful owner. The question of what to do with the ranch was under consideration.

Four weeks after the day of the trial at Black Creek, a stranger rode into Brody from the north, in the afternoon. His name was Ellison. He was a broad, squat man, bearded and swarthy, dressed in the normal garb of a trail hand. He dismounted at the saloon and went inside. He walked up to the bar and regarded the barkeep with what he hoped was an affable smile. But the smile did not sit easy on the dark, bleak face.

'I've had a long thirsty ride,' he said. 'A beer would be good. And maybe more than one.'

The bar was almost empty, and as he drank his beer the stranger chatted with the barkeep, telling him that he was on the way back to San Antonio after helping to drive a trail herd up to Dodge City.

'When I stayed for a night in Amarillo,' he said, 'I heard tell of a big ruckus down this way. Something about a man called Sinclair, I think that was the name, who gunned down four outlaws. Must have caused quite a stir here when it all happened.'

'It sure did,' said the barkeep, a naturally loquacious man who found pleasure in chatting to the customers when business was slack. 'From all accounts, Sinclair's mighty handy with a six-gun. He saved all the folks on the Crazy L from being killed. He's still working on the ranch. I heard that he and Marian Lee, the rancher's daughter, are aiming to get married. Don't know when.'

'That's a real romantic story,' said Ellison. 'Stranger rides into town, saves a woman's life by gunning down four outlaws, and they get hitched. And let's hope they live happy ever after. I'd admire to meet this Sinclair and shake him by the hand.'

'If you stay on here till tomorrow afternoon, you might get the chance,' said the barkeep. 'That's the day he usually comes in on the buckboard with Marian Lee to pick up supplies at the store.'

'Darn it!' said Ellison, 'I'd like to do that, but I just ain't got the time to stay here overnight. I'm heading out of town right now.'

Ellison finished his second beer, then left the saloon. He made a few purchases at the general store, then rode south out of town. After a mile he headed east, and eleven miles on he rode into a small gully, a little way off the trail. Seated by a camp fire in the bottom of the gully, Nolan and Radford rose to their feet as he rode up to them and dismounted.

'Had any luck?' asked Nolan, who had recruited Ellison to his gang, and had also persuaded Radford to return by offering him a larger share of the proceeds of their criminal activities.

'I sure have,' said Ellison, and went on to tell the others what he had learnt from the barkeep.

'Right,' said Nolan. 'It looks like we can make our move tomorrow. So far as we can tell, there are no lawmen around here just now. So we'll ambush Sinclair tomorrow, either on his way to town in the buckboard or on his way back. I know the route he'll be taking. It passes by a grove of trees big enough for us to hide in with the horses. We'll shoot Sinclair from cover with our rifles. Then we'll head for the Indian Territory.'

'How about the woman?' asked Ellison.

'We'd better make a clean job of it,' Nolan replied. 'We don't want to leave no witness behind. We'll shoot the woman down as well. Best time for the ambush will be when they're on their way into town. That way, it'll be longer before they're missed at the ranch. So we'll go into the grove before daybreak. We'll hide the bodies in the middle of the trees, with the buckboard and the horses. Should be quite a while before they're found. By then, we'll be well on our way to the border.'

10

On the Crazy L, on the morning of the day after Ellison's arrival in Brody, Rob was talking to Marian after they had finished breakfast.

'We'd better go to Brody tomorrow instead of today,' he said. 'We've got a lot of sick cows out on the range. I reckon I should help Luke and Hank treat them.'

'You do that,' said Marian. 'I'll drive the buckboard in myself. I'm looking forward to seeing my friend Jane Bellamy. She's the daughter of the storekeeper in Brody. She's just got back from a stay with relatives in Kansas City.'

'I don't feel too easy about you driving into Brody alone,' said Rob.

'I'll be all right,' she said. 'I reckon you've taken care of all the bad men around here. And I've got lots to tell

Jane, and I'm sure she's got lots to tell me.'

Marian left for Brody half an hour later. Watching from just inside the grove, Nolan and his companions saw the buckboard approaching. Observing it through field glasses, Nolan cursed.

'Damn!' he said. 'I see Lee's daughter. But she's alone. Sinclair's not with her.'

His mind working quickly, he watched the approaching buckboard.

'Change of plan,' he said. 'We'll take the woman prisoner and use her to get our hands on Sinclair. I've got an idea how we can do that.'

As the buckboard passed close to the edge of the grove the three men ran out in front of it with six-guns in their hands. The horses reared, then came to a stop as Marian brought them under control. Her heart sank as she recognised Nolan as he walked up to speak to her.

'You'll be coming with us,' he said. 'We aim to use you to get hold of the man you were going to marry. He's due to pay for killing two of my men.'

'He's got the better of you once,' said Marian, defiantly, 'and he'll do it again.' But she knew there was a strong possibility that both she and Rob would die.

'Not this time,' said Nolan. 'Sinclair is finished for sure.'

Marian remained silent as the buckboard was taken into the grove and she was ordered to climb down. Nolan took the small bag lying on the buckboard seat and looked inside it. From it he took some banknotes, together with a pencil and a sheet of paper on which Marian had listed the items required from the store. On the back of this sheet he wrote a message. He left this on the seat, with a stone on top to hold it down.

A horse was unhitched from the buckboard. Marian's hands were tied and she was helped on to this. Riding bareback, she was led off to the east by Turner, accompanied by Nolan and Radford.

* * *

It was around four in the afternoon when Lee saw Rob and the two hands returning from their mission to treat the sick cattle. He spoke to them as they rode up to the ranch house.

'I'm worried about Marian,' he said. 'I know she was going to see her friend in Brody, but even allowing for that I reckon she should be back by now.'

'Maybe the buckboard's broke down,' said Rob. 'I'll ride towards Brody and see if she needs any help.'

He left immediately, and as he came in sight of Brody without seeing any sign of Marian he grew more and more concerned. Riding into town, he quickly discovered that Marian had not been seen there that day. He rode back towards the ranch, searching the area on either side of the trail for any sign of Marian and the buckboard.

Reaching the grove he rode inside it and discovered the buckboard, with one horse still hitched to it. Frantically, he searched the grove for Marian. There was no sign of her. He returned to the buckboard. The sheet of paper on the seat caught his eye. He picked it up and looked at the message. It read:

I have the woman, Sinclair. But the one I want is you. Tomorrow, that's Wednesday, you'll ride alone to Comanche Bluff east of here. Ride up to the bluff at exactly two hours after noon and give yourself up. Do this and the woman will be set free with a horse. If you don't turn up or if anyone is seen following you, the woman dies. Nolan.

Badly shocked, Rob read the message twice. Then, leaving the buckboard and horse to be picked up by Hank or Luke later, he rode off fast to the Crazy L ranch house. He showed the message to Lee and the hands, explaining where he had found it. They were all deeply worried.

'You'll be doing like they say?' asked Lee.

'First,' said Rob, 'does anybody know how far it is from here to Comanche Bluff?'

'It's fifty miles or more east of here,' said Hank. 'I passed it a while back when I was visiting some kinfolk in the Indian Territory. Actually climbed up it to see the view from the top. It stands on its own in the middle of a big area of flat ground.'

At Rob's request, Hank described the bluff and the area around it as well as his memory of the occasion allowed.

'One thing's clear to me,' said Rob. 'We know that Nolan has no qualms about killing. We were all due to die in that cave. So even if I do what he wants, he'll never free Marian. He'll kill us both.'

'I think you're right,' said Lee, deeply concerned over the danger his daughter was facing. 'So what do we do?'

'If I set off right now on the best horse we've got on the ranch,' said Rob, 'I might just be able to reach Comanche Bluff long enough before daybreak to be able to hide on it without being seen. Maybe Nolan and the others will be on the bluff when I get there. Maybe they aim to reach it after daybreak. Either way, I'll try to hide on the bluff so I can surprise Nolan and the others and set Marian free.'

'All right,' said Lee, and asked Luke to saddle the rancher's own big chestnut for the ride to the bluff.

Rob rode off fifteen minutes later, after getting information from Hank about landmarks on the route. When darkness fell he navigated with the help of these landmarks and the North Star. Fearful of what Marian may be enduring, he rode on steadily during the night, with occasional brief periods of rest. It was still dark when, ahead of him, silhouetted against the night sky, he saw the looming bulk of Comanche Bluff.

Hank had told him that the sloping side of the bluff was too steep for a horse to climb. Rob dismounted, picketed his horse, then approached the bluff cautiously on foot. It did not take him long to discover that there were no horses anywhere round the foot of the bluff. He returned to the chestnut and headed for a low ridge half a mile to the east, about which he had been told by Hank. He picketed his horse on the far side of this ridge, then ran back to the bluff, carrying field glasses, his rifle and six-gun and a good supply of ammunition.

There were still no horses at the bluff. He climbed up the west-facing slope which was scattered with large, partly embedded boulders. He settled down behind one of these to watch out for any sign of Marian and her captors. The sky was lightening in the east.

His vigil was rewarded six hours later when he saw two riders in the distance, approaching from the west. He trained the field glasses on them, and as they drew closer he could see that the riders were Marian and Radford. He guessed that Nolan and Radford had joined up after Nolan had left the Circle Dot. He wondered whether Nolan had any other men with him. He suspected that the outlaw might be hiding somewhere to the west with the intention of watching out for his arrival and checking that he was alone.

The two riders reached the bluff, then partially circled it and dismounted on the east side. Rob followed them round, keeping under cover. He saw Marian sit down on the ground. Radford also sat down but Rob's view of him was blocked by one of the horses. There was no cover on the steep slope below Rob and the surface was scattered with loose stones. The distance was too great for accurate pistol shooting. The best possible way of ensuring Marian's safety, he thought, would be to despatch Radford by a single accurately aimed rifle bullet.

He took hold of his Winchester and adjusted the sight. Then he stood watching and waiting for the opportunity to fire the lethal shot, hoping fervently that he could do this well before the arrival of Nolan or any other member of the gang. After a short while Marian shifted her position on the ground and looked up the slope in Rob's direction. He stepped out from behind the boulder and waved the arm which was holding his rifle. He did this long enough to ensure that Marian had recognized him. Then he stepped back out of sight.

At the totally unexpected sight of Rob, Marian felt a surge of hope. She stifled an involuntary cry and looked towards Radford, several yards away. He was sitting on the ground looking away from the bluff, still out of Rob's view. She knew that somehow she had to get him into a position where Rob would have a clear view of him. She got up and walked away from the outlaw, towards the foot of the slope. He got up and, moving away from the horse, took a couple of steps in her direction. He was carrying his rifle.

'Hold it!' he shouted. 'Where d'you

reckon you're going? You only move when *I* say so.'

Marian halted. 'Just stretching my legs,' she said, then sat down again. Radford, facing the bluff, stood looking at her.

Up the slope, Rob steadied himself against the side of the boulder. The air was still. He drew a careful bead on the outlaw's chest and fired. He watched as Radford staggered backwards, fell to the ground, and lay motionless. Marian ran up to take the outlaw's six-gun and pick up his rifle.

Hastily, Rob moved down the slope and confirmed that the outlaw was dead. He took Marian in his arms. He could feel her trembling. 'You all right, Marian?' he asked.

'I'm all right,' she said. 'They didn't harm me. Nolan's out there somewhere with another man called Ellison. They were going to come here before you were due to turn up.'

'They might have heard that rifle shot,' said Rob. 'We can't get away from here fast enough. The main thing now is to get you safely back to the ranch.'

Rob ran round the bluff to look towards the west. He could see no sign of riders approaching. He ran back to Marian and using the mounts on which she and Radford had arrived at the bluff they rode east to the place where Rob had left the chestnut. Marian was riding Radford's horse. Rob transferred to the chestnut and, leading the Crazy L horse on which Marian had arrived at the bluff, they rode along the foot of the ridge towards the north, out of sight of the bluff. After covering two miles they swung west and embarked on the long ride to the Crazy L. Using the food and drink which Rob had brought with him, they made steady progress and reached the ranch during the evening. There had been no sign of Nolan and Ellison.

Lee's relief at the sight of his daughter was intense. 'I figured there weren't much chance of seeing either of you back here again,' he said. 'What happened?'

Marian and Rob described to Lee and the two hands the events following the capture of Marian.

'It looks,' said Rob, 'like Nolan was mighty riled about losing Turner and Haley. Now he's going to be even more riled that he's lost Radford as well. I don't reckon I need to look for him. I think he's so mad he'll have another try at getting me. I don't want to put you folks in danger. Maybe I'd better stay in Brody for the time being.'

'No!' said Marian. 'You'll be safer here with the four of us.'

'Marian's right,' said her father. 'And what if Nolan gets the notion to kidnap Marian again. We need you here.'

'All right,' said Rob. 'We'll carry on as we did before, with a night guard posted.'

★　★　★

A little over two hours after Rob and Marian rode away from Comanche Bluff, Nolan and Ellison rode up from the west. They had been watching out for Rob's approach at the specified time. After waiting an hour without any sign of him or other riders, they had decided to rejoin Radford and the prisoner. They rode a little way round the foot of the bluff, then stopped short as they came upon the body of Radford. There was no sign of the prisoner or the horses. They dismounted, and Ellison checked that Radford had been shot dead. Nolan exploded with rage.

'This is Sinclair's doing,' he said. 'I'm sure of it. He took a risk and it paid off. And that makes three of my men he's killed. I guess that he and the woman are well on the way to the Crazy L by now. There's no hope of us catching them. But one thing's certain. I'll get Sinclair. And when I do get him he won't die easy.'

11

After discovering the dead body of Radford, Nolan and Ellison rode to a hideout in a secluded ravine, north-east of Comanche Bluff, and not far from the border with the Indian Territory. On the evening of the following day Nolan left Ellison at the hideout and rode into the Indian Territory. He had several contacts there who might help him in his desire to restore his depleted gang to its previous size. The Indian Territory was an obvious place for a search of this nature because it was a haven for criminals fleeing from the law in the surrounding states.

Nolan was well known throughout the criminal fraternity as a first-class planner of criminal operations. From robberies carried out over a number of years he had amassed a considerable amount, all safely stashed away. So within four days he was successful in recruiting to his gang two men, Gummer and Emery. Both were hardened criminals, wanted by the law, normally operating as a pair. Nolan told them that his first objective was the killing of Sinclair, and promised them a handsome bonus for their help in this operation. They agreed to join him and Ellison at the hideout over the border three days later. Nolan headed back to rejoin Ellison and await their arrival.

Soon after crossing the border into the Texas Panhandle, late in the afternoon, he saw the small settlement of Buffalo Spring off to his right. It boasted no more than half a dozen buildings, including a general store. Nolan paused. He needed some tobacco. He had never operated in this area, and he figured it most unlikely that anybody in the settlement would recognize him. He headed for the buildings.

When he arrived at the settlement the street was deserted. Two horses were standing outside the small saloon. He rode to the store, dismounted, and went inside. Half a minute earlier, as he had ridden slowly past the saloon, Texas Ranger Colby, who had captured Vickery and his men on the Circle Dot, was sitting with his partner Anderson at a table by one of the windows. The two lawmen had been on a patrol along the border, and their orders had been that when they arrived at Buffalo Spring they should then ride straight to Amarillo to join a posse for an operation in the north of the Texas Panhandle.

Colby glanced out of the window as Nolan was passing. He stiffened and studied the rider closely. There was no doubt in his mind that he was looking at Nolan, who had avoided capture for so long. He rose quickly and spoke urgently to his partner.

Inside the store, Nolan completed his purchase, pulled open the door and walked out on to the boardwalk. Confronted by the two rangers, he stopped short, his hand moving towards his six-gun. But the sight of the shotgun held by Colby and pointing at his belly halted the move. He raised his hands.

'This is a great day for law and order, Nolan,' said Colby. 'You and your men have been robbing and killing far too long. Me and my partner are heading for Amarillo. We'll take you with us. That's where you'll be tried, and I guess that's where you'll hang. And don't you get the idea that maybe you can escape on the way. Neither me or my partner has ever lost a prisoner yet. And one or other of us will be watching you all the time, with a loaded shotgun handy.'

Nolan made no comment as Anderson handcuffed him and took his six-gun.

* * *

The two rangers reached Amarillo with their prisoner, without incident. They reported to Ranger Captain Emerson who had Nolan put into a jail cell in a room behind his office.

'This is quite a catch,' said Emerson. 'Marshal Kennedy will want to hear about this. He asked me to let him know if there were any sightings of Nolan. I'll walk along and tell him right now. You two will be riding north in the morning.'

The captain walked along the street to the US marshal's office and went inside. Kennedy was seated at a desk. Emerson gave him the good news.

'I told you all about Sinclair and his search for Nolan and his gang,' said Kennedy. 'I've only just heard from him that he killed Radford at Comanche Bluff, not far from Buffalo Spring. He said that Nolan and a man called Ellison were in the area around Comanche Bluff at the time, but he has no idea where they are now. So Nolan's the only one left of the gang that killed Sinclair's parents. I've got to let him know we've got Nolan in jail. I'll send a message to him today to tell him that he can stop searching. The judge is sick right now, but according to the doctor he'll be fit in two or three weeks. Till then you'll have to hold Nolan in jail.'

*   *   *

When Rob received the message from Marshal Kennedy, there was great relief on the Crazy L. The wedding was arranged for ten days ahead and a telegraph message was sent to Rob's sister Elizabeth, inviting her to attend. She arrived by stagecoach five days later. She and Marian took an instant liking to one another.

Now that the wedding was imminent, Rob and Marian were giving serious consideration to their future. The thought came to Rob that perhaps they could buy the Circle Dot. It was a fair-sized ranch, but they could start in a small way and gradually expand. And the arrangement would meet Marian's wish to be near her father. He put the idea to Marian and it was enthusiastically approved. So he started making enquiries to Fort Worth about his possible purchase of the Circle Dot. He already knew that Vickery had no known heirs.

As for Elizabeth, she was as yet undecided whether she wanted to move from Cheyenne to join Rob and Marian on a permanent basis.

*　*　*

Two days after Nolan was captured by the rangers in Buffalo Spring, Gummer and Emery rode up to the hideout ravine in the Texas Panhandle, the location of which had been given to them by Nolan. They rode into the small ravine with hands raised. Ellison, who had seen them approaching, stood with a six-gun in his hand as they rode up to him. Recognizing the two men, whom he had once met briefly in the Indian Territory, he holstered his weapon.

'Where's Nolan?' he asked.

'We figured he was here,' said

Gummer. 'He left us two days ago. Said he was riding back here. We told him we'd join up with him here today.'

'Well, he never turned up,' said Ellison. 'I don't like this. We'll wait till tomorrow morning, then I'll ride into Buffalo Spring and see if there's any talk about him there.'

When Nolan had not turned up the following morning, Ellison rode into Buffalo Spring, leaving the other two men in the ravine. Arriving there, he went into the general store, ostensibly to buy a few supplies. It was not difficult to get the information he was seeking. Without any prompting, the storekeeper gave him a graphic description of the capture of the notorious outlaw Nolan by two Texas Rangers who just happened to be in the town. Ellison also learnt that Nolan had been taken to Amarillo by the two lawmen to face trial. He returned to the ravine and gave the bad news to Gummer and Emery. They all sat down to discuss the situation in which they now found themselves.

'I know,' said Ellison, 'that Nolan has a considerable heap of money stashed away somewhere. I figure he'd be mighty grateful to us if we got him out of jail. I reckon the three of us could manage it. And when he's free, the four of us could start operating as a gang, with Nolan providing the brains. What d'you think?'

'I reckon it's worth a try,' said Gummer, 'but we're going to need some brain power ourselves to think up a plan to get Nolan out of that jail in Amarillo.'

'I'll go along with you two,' said Emery.

'Right,' said Ellison. 'I know a hideout we can use not far from Amarillo. We'll ride there and buy a horse for Nolan on the way. Then one of you can ride in to Amarillo and check up on the situation there. Is either of you wanted for crimes committed in Texas?'

They both shook their heads.

'It had better be one of you, then,'

said Ellison. 'I'm too well known in this state to show myself in Amarillo.'

They arrived at the hideout late the following day. It was a deep gully, about fourteen miles from Amarillo, well away from the main trails in the area.

The following morning Gummer rode to Amarillo, with the intention of returning to the gully when he had sufficient information to enable them to decide on a plan to break Nolan out of jail. On his arrival there he took a room at the hotel on the opposite side of the street from Ranger Captain Emerson's office. His room looked out on the street below, with a clear view of the office.

He left the hotel, handed his horse in at the livery stable, then walked to the nearest saloon. An hour later, after buying drinks for several of the customers, and without putting any direct questions which might give rise to suspicion, he was in possession of some valuable pieces of information. Nolan was in a jail cell behind Captain

Emerson's office. The trial was delayed because of the illness of the judge. And US Marshal Kennedy had been suddenly struck down the previous evening by a mysterious illness which had produced a high fever, had put him in an unconscious state, and was threatening his life.

'I've heard a lot about this outlaw Nolan,' said Gummer. 'A cold killer is what I heard. I expect he's pretty well guarded.'

'He sure is,' said one of the customers, who was employed to clean the captain's office and the cells. 'When the office closes down for the night around nine o'clock, Ranger Parker comes on duty.'

He pointed to a youngish man who had been sitting at a table, and was now leaving the saloon. 'That's Parker,' he said. 'He locks the doors and guards the cells all night with a shotgun.'

Gummer went back to the hotel, where he took a meal, then went up to his room and sat by the window observing the activities down below. He had been sitting there thirty minutes when he saw Ranger Parker walking along the boardwalk on the opposite side of the street. He was accompanied by a young woman and a boy aged about five. Gummer watched them as they went into the store next to Captain Emerson's office. They came out twenty minutes later and walked back along the street out of Gummer's view. He opened the window and leaned out, just in time to see them entering a small house along the street. He closed the window and returned to his chair.

Two hours later he saw four Texas Rangers ride up to the office. A man who Gummer took to be Captain Emerson came out of the office and spoke for a short while to the four rangers. Then he went inside again and the four men rode off.

Gummer left the hotel. Looking along the street, he saw Parker carrying out some repairs on the fence outside the house he had previously entered.

The woman was sitting in the small garden. The boy was playing nearby. Gummer walked across the street and entered the alley between the store and the adjoining house, which belonged to the doctor. He walked out of the far end of the alley and looked towards the rear of Emerson's office. He could see a door in the back wall of the building. He returned through the alley and went to his hotel room. So far as he could tell his movements had not been observed.

He continued his surveillance, and around seven in the evening he saw Captain Emerson leave his office and disappear from view. He went downstairs for a hurried meal and returned to his room half an hour later. At nine o'clock, by the light of a lamp hanging outside the building, he saw Parker enter the office and shortly after this two rangers came out and walked away. Gummer decided it would be a good idea to get some sleep.

The following morning, after breakfast, he paid his hotel bill and rode to the hideout. He told the others everything he had learnt in Amarillo. Then the three of them had a long discussion over the tactics to be used in breaking Nolan out of jail. Finally they reached agreement.

Later in the day they all rode away from the gully, leading the horse to be used by Nolan. They arrived outside Amarillo at around eight o'clock in the evening. Darkness was falling. Ellison and Emery dismounted. After a few words with the others, Gummer rode on towards town. He approached Ranger Parker's house from the rear, dismounted a short distance away, and tied his horse to a post. He walked up to the back door of the house. It was not fastened. He opened it and slipped into the kitchen. He could see a light underneath a door leading to the living room. He could hear the murmur of voices. He drew his six-gun, turned the door handle, flung the door open, and stepped inside the room.

Parker was seated at a table, with his

wife and son. Taken completely by surprise, he started to rise, then saw the six-gun in the intruder's hand. He sank back on his chair. Frightened, his wife and son stared at Gummer.

'There's something you've got to do for me and my partners, Parker,' said Gummer. 'We know you're going to guard Nolan in the jail overnight. What you have to do at exactly one hour after midnight is open the back door of the jail to let my partners in. Then you'll open the cell door and let Nolan out.

'I think you're going to do this for us because if you don't, I'm going to have to kill your wife and boy. You can go on duty at nine as usual, but I'll stay on here till I hear from my partners that Nolan is free. Then I'll leave without harming your family. Any tricks, any attempts to save them, and they die. I'll have a gun on them the whole time.'

Parker looked into the hard, ruthless face of Gummer. He was convinced the man was not bluffing.

'Damn you!' he said. 'I'll do what you

want. But if you harm my wife and boy no lawman is going to rest until you're caught.'

Parker spoke to his wife and son. He told them to stay calm and not cause the intruder any trouble. He said to stay in the house till he came back the following morning. Then he left the house, gravely concerned about what the night might bring. He entered the captain's office. The two rangers there were getting ready to leave. One of them looked closely at Parker's face.

'You don't look too good,' he said. 'I'll do the night watch for you if you like.'

'Thanks,' said Parker, 'but there's no need. I'll be all right. A bit of a headache is all.'

The two rangers left and Parker fastened the door behind them. Then he walked into the jail area which, like the office, was lit by an oil lamp. Nolan was lying on a bunk in one of the cells. The other two were empty. Parker checked that the rear door was fastened then returned to the office. He sat down on a chair, acutely aware of the dilemma he faced and the decision he had been forced to take.

Just before one o'clock he rose from the chair and walked into the jail. Curious, Nolan watched him as he unbolted the rear door and opened it. A moment later, as he saw Emery and Ellison enter, he rose quickly from the bunk and ran to the door of the cell.

'Open the cell door,' said Ellison to Parker. The ranger took a key from his pocket and unlocked the door. As he was straightening up Emery struck him on the back of his head with the barrel of his six-gun. His hands and feet were securely tied. He was gagged and dragged into the cell. Nolan removed the ranger's gunbelt and pistol and buckled it on himself. As the door was being locked on Parker, he was showing signs of coming to.

'There's a horse waiting outside for you,' said Ellison to Nolan. 'And Gummer will be joining up with us shortly. We'd best be moving.'

They left the building and ran towards the waiting horses.

★ ★ ★

At two hours after midnight, in Parker's house, Gummer spoke to Parker's wife, who was with him in the living room. The boy was sitting by her side.

'I'm leaving now,' he said. 'But you take heed of what your husband told you. Stay here till he comes back. If you leave here and raise a ruckus, you won't see him alive again.'

He left the house and went to his horse. Riding along the backs of the buildings, he joined up with Nolan and the others behind the jail. With Nolan leading, they rode out of town in a westerly direction.

'Where are we heading?' asked Ellison.

'We're leaving tracks which could give them the idea that we're heading for New Mexico Territory,' said Nolan.

'But after six miles or so we ride onto ground where they can't follow our tracks. Then we'll swing south and head for the Crazy L. We ain't going to rest till Sinclair's finished for good. And I ain't going to forget what you three just did for me.'

It was not until eight o'clock in the morning, when two rangers turned up to relieve Parker, that the escape of the prisoner was discovered. Parker had a sore head but was otherwise all right. He rushed to his house to find that his wife and son were unharmed.

A posse was organized and the tracks of Nolan and the others were followed for six miles in a westerly direction. But then they were lost, and despite an intensive search lasting two days no further trace of the outlaws was found. The posse returned to Amarillo.

US Marshal Kennedy was still hovering between life and death.

12

The wedding of Rob and Marian was held in the small church in Brody, with the preacher conducting the ceremony. Many townspeople were present. The bride was given away by her father, now almost fully recovered from his gunshot wound. Everyone moved to the hotel where refreshments were laid on. The bride and groom stayed the night at the hotel and rode back to the Crazy L the following morning.

In the afternoon, Marian and Elizabeth decided to go for a ride in the surrounding area. Lee was out on the range with the two hands and Rob had some chores to attend to in the barn. It was a hot day and Marian told Rob that they were riding to a deep pool in a river, about five miles away, where they would be able to swim.

'I'd sure like to come with you,' said

Rob, who knew the place, 'but this work just has to be done. Don't stay out too long.'

An hour after the two women had ridden off Rob was walking out of the barn when he saw a rider approaching from the north at a fast pace. He stood waiting and recognised the rider as Doc Fender, from Brody. He was surprised because Fender normally rode around in a buggy. The horse came to a halt and the doctor dismounted. He was breathing heavily.

'Rob,' he said. 'I've got some bad news for you. Figured you needed to hear it just as soon as I could bring it here. I got it from a drummer in Brody who was in Amarillo a few days ago. While he was there, Nolan escaped from jail. Three men helped to break him out. Nobody knows who they were. A posse went after them, but the gang disappeared without trace.'

'This is real bad news,' said Rob. 'I have a feeling that Nolan and the others may be somewhere in this area. I know that Nolan is dead set on killing me. And Marian and Elizabeth have ridden off alone to a pool not far from here for a swim. I'm real worried they might meet up with Nolan and the others. I'm riding out there right now as fast as I can. I'd be obliged if you'd wait here and let Marian's father know what's happened when he gets back. He's somewhere out on the range with Hank and Luke, but I don't know exactly where. Tell him about the pool. He knows where it is.'

He ran for his six-gun and rifle, then his horse, which he saddled, and rode off at the fastest speed of which his mount was capable. As he was approaching the pool, he caught sight of a distant group of riders to the south. He pulled up behind a large boulder and looked at them. He could see that there were six riders, but they were too distant for him to identify any of them. As he watched, the riders disappeared out of sight as they rode through a narrow gap in a low ridge running across their path.

Quickly, Rob rode on to the pool and dismounted. There was no sign of his wife and sister. But in the soft ground around the edge of the pool there were the fresh tracks of a number of horses, certainly more than two, and the footprints of a corresponding number of people. Rob now faced the strong possibility that Marian and Elizabeth were in the hands of Nolan and his gang.

He mounted, and rode quickly to the gap in the ridge through which the six riders had disappeared. He rode up to the gap and through it. He took cover at the far end and scanned the terrain ahead. He was just in time to see the riders skirting a small grove of trees in the distance. Then they disappeared from view. He followed the riders in this fashion, taking what precautions he could to avoid being seen.

He guessed they had covered around twenty miles during which there were several slight changes of direction when, watching from cover, he saw the six riders enter a small ravine from which they did not emerge. He guessed that this was being used as a hideout, and that they had probably stationed a lookout. He would have to wait until darkness fell before he could get any closer.

He had not long to wait. As soon as he judged it was dark enough, he rode towards the ravine. Avoiding the entrance, he approached the top of one of the sides. He dismounted a little way off and ran to a point from which he could look into the ravine. He lay there and looked down searchingly into the darkness. Almost directly below him he saw the dim glow of a campfire. And he heard the faint sound of voices. He guessed that a guard could have been posted somewhere near the lower end of the ravine. He decided to make his way down to the bottom of the ravine and investigate. He found a small hollow nearby, where he hid and secured his horse. Then he carefully made his way down the side of the ravine well upwards of the location of the campfire. There were numerous boulders and patches of brush scattered along the floor and the sides of the ravine. Rob took full advantage of these as he worked his way towards the campfire.

He passed fairly close to the horses, fastened to a picket line. There were six of them, and two of these looked similar to the ones on which Marian and Elizabeth had ridden off earlier in the day. But in the darkness he could not be sure. With infinite caution, he worked his way towards a group of three men sitting by the campfire. He ended up standing behind a boulder, close enough to the group to be just able to hear most of what they were saying.

He looked around for the two captives. Then, as the fire flared up he saw them lying on the ground, side by side, and bound hand and foot. They were just out of earshot of the men by the fire. Rob identified one of these as Nolan. The other two were strangers to him. He assumed that the missing man was on guard somewhere down the ravine. He strained to hear the conversation. Fortuitously, Nolan was outlining to the other two his plans for the gang in the immediate future.

'We just had a big stroke of luck,' he said, 'meeting up with Sinclair's wife and her friend like that. Like we planned to do before, we can use her to get our hands on Sinclair himself. But this time there won't be no mistakes. I'm going to ride off soon to make sure that a message gets to Sinclair telling him just what he has to do. We should be safe here for a short while. The way we came, nobody would be able to track us, except maybe an Indian. I'll be back here in about four hours.

'When we've finally dealt with Sinclair we'll ride to Archer's place at Tresco in the Indian Territory. I feel like resting up for a while before we start operating again.'

'I've heard of Archer's place,' said Emery. 'Ain't it a big saloon with plenty of girls and gaming?'

'That's right,' said Nolan. 'And it's a good safe place for us to hide from the law. I'm going to leave now. Keep a close watch on the women. And don't forget to relieve Ellison a couple of hours from now.'

Nolan rode off a few minutes later and Rob heard the faint shouted exchange of words as he passed the lookout. Rob moved from the boulder and slowly worked his way down the ravine, listening and watching for any indication of where the lookout was located. He thought he heard a cough coming from the top of the wall at the mouth of the ravine. Cautiously, he moved towards the sound, and a moment later the flare of a match as Ellison lit a cigarette gave Rob his exact location.

Rob knew that the lives of himself and his wife and sister depended on his actions during the next half hour or so. The lookout must be dealt with silently to avoid alerting the others. He drew his knife from his belt and slowly and silently he moved forward through the darkness. He came up behind Ellison, who was standing beside a large boulder, and drove the knife blade deep into the outlaw's back. It was a lethal thrust and Ellison collapsed on the ground with just a brief strangled cry of shock and pain. Rob retrieved his knife, then moved back to his previous position behind the boulder near the campfire. Emery and Gummer were still sitting in the same position, chatting in a desultory fashion. The two women were still lying in the same place.

Rob moved back to the horses. He untied from the picket line one of the horses belonging to the outlaws. Then, with the horse between him and the two men at the fire, he ran alongside the animal, leading it past Gummer and Emery. In the darkness they could see the horse, but not Rob.

Cursing, both men jumped to their feet. 'Damn Ellison,' said Emery. 'I've told him before about not tying up the horses right.'

He left Gummer and ran after the horse. Rob ran with it for about forty yards, then released it to run on a little further on its own. He turned to face Emery, who was fast approaching. The outlaw saw the figure of Rob looming up in the darkness ahead and stopped abruptly. He could tell that the man in front of him was neither Ellison nor Nolan. He drew his six-gun. But before he had levelled it and cocked the hammer a bullet from Rob's Peacemaker penetrated his heart. Rob ran past him towards the fire, and stopped when he saw Gummer, alerted by the shot, coming towards him. Gummer met the same fate as his partner. Seeing the stranger, he brought his six-gun up to bear on Rob, but before he could fire he also was struck in the heart.

Rob bent briefly over the two men lying on the ground, then picked up their weapons. He went for the horse and ran back with it to the picket line, where he secured it. Then he hurried to the two women lying on the ground. Staring into the darkness, wondering about the shooting, they saw Rob approaching.

'It's Rob,' he said, as he knelt down and untied their hands and feet. 'Three of the outlaws won't bother us no more. And I happen to know that Nolan ain't due back here for a while.'

'I'm getting tired of being kidnapped,' said Marian, trying to smile. But her voice was shaky and she was trembling a little.

'Are you two all right?' asked Rob.

'Up to now they haven't harmed us,' said Marian, 'but we didn't know how long that was going to last. Can we head back home now?'

'We could,' said Rob, 'but before we do there's something I have to ask you both. Nolan is due back here in around three and a half hours from now. From what's been happening it looks like he's absolutely set on killing me, and maybe Marian as well. I think I should wait for him here, and settle this matter once and for all. Otherwise, we'll never be able to rest easy, knowing he's still on the loose. So I was hoping you wouldn't mind staying on here with me till he gets back. But if you'd sooner we all left now, then that's what we'll do.'

'I think we should stay,' said Marian. 'Maybe this will be the best chance we get of ridding ourselves of Nolan.'

'I agree with that,' said Elizabeth. 'I haven't forgotten the day Nolan was responsible for the deaths of my father and mother. What can we do to help you?'

'I think,' said Rob, impressed by the composure of his sister after such an ordeal, 'that the safest way to do this would be for me to wait for Nolan near the entrance to the ravine. He's bound to stop there to hail the lookout. You two can hide out of sight somewhere around here. You'll both be carrying a pistol just in case Nolan gets past me. But I just can't see that happening. He won't be expecting any trouble.'

During a short discussion, Rob persuaded the two women that his proposed course of action was the best that could be taken. Then he hid the bodies of the three outlaws and rejoined his wife and sister. They all had a meal, using the provisions the outlaws had brought with them.

'I'd best go now,' said Rob after the meal, 'in case Nolan gets back early for any reason. You two can take cover behind those boulders near the fire. If he hasn't turned up by the time he said he would, I'll wait another ninety minutes, and if he still hasn't turned up I'll come back here.'

He left them and found a hiding place near the entrance to the ravine, close to the point where Nolan would be likely to stop and hail the lookout. But the hours passed without any sign of him, and an hour and a half after the time of Nolan's expected arrival Rob went back to Marian and Elizabeth.

'I don't understand it,' he said. 'Maybe he just got held up. Maybe he somehow got wind of the fact that we've set a trap for him. Maybe he's hanging around, aiming to take some shots at us. I reckon that now, while it's still dark, we should leave here and head for the ranch. When we get there we'll arrange for the bodies here to be picked up.'

They left shortly after, leading the horses belonging to the three dead outlaws. They arrived at the Crazy L without incident.

★　★　★

When Nolan left the ravine he was carrying a message in a sealed envelope. It was addressed to Rob and gave instructions on how Rob was to give himself up so as to obtain the release of his wife and the woman with her. The outlaw rode to a homestead about nine miles from the Crazy L. No lights were showing from inside the house. He hammered on the door. It was opened shortly after by Gleason, the home-steader, holding a lamp in his hand. He looked closely at the stranger.

'You know the Crazy L?' asked Nolan. 'It's owned by a man called Lee.'

'Sure,' said Gleason. 'Mr Lee done me a good turn or two in the past.'

'I have an urgent message for a man called Sinclair who's staying there,' said Nolan. 'I can't take it myself. I was hoping you'd take it for me.'

'I know Sinclair,' said the homesteader. 'Met him a few times in Brody. I don't know what this is all about, but if you reckon it's so urgent I'll ride over there at daybreak.'

'That'll do fine,' said Nolan, and handed the message over.

He left the homestead and headed towards the ravine. He was about halfway there when, in the darkness, his horse stepped into a hole. He was thrown out of the saddle. He fell awkwardly, twisting his leg, and his head hit the hard ground. He was stunned for a short time. When he came to, he rose slowly to his feet and limped over to his horse which was standing close by. He soon established that one of its forelegs was so badly damaged that it could not possibly carry him any further. Drawing his six-gun, he shot the animal dead. Then he considered his plight. He had no option but to walk the rest of the way to the ravine. Carrying his saddlebags and rifle he limped off in that direction.

By the time he reached his destination the sky was lightening in the east and the pain in his leg was intense. He stopped at the entrance to the ravine and hailed the lookout. He did this several times, but there was no response. Drawing his pistol he limped cautiously into the ravine and, moving from cover to cover, he made his way along it. There was no sign of his men, the prisoners, or the five horses which had been standing at the picket line when he left. A search of the ravine revealed the bodies of the three members of his gang.

It was clear to him now that the two

women had escaped, taking all the horses with them. But they must have had help, possibly from Sinclair. It was likely that men would be out looking for him before long. He must get a horse as quickly as possible and head for the Indian Territory. He left the ravine, carrying his rifle and saddle-bags, and limped off painfully towards the east.

13

When Rob arrived at the Crazy L ranch house with Marian and Elizabeth, Lee and the two hands, who were waiting there, were greatly relieved. They had gone to the pool but had found no sign of Rob and the women, and were unable to follow the tracks. So they had returned to the ranch to await news from Rob. As they were talking, the homesteader Gleason rode up with the message from Nolan.

Rob read it and passed it to the others. 'Just the same as when Marian was kidnapped,' he observed. 'I go alone to a remote place, give myself up, and Marian and Elizabeth will be freed to ride back to the ranch. I can't think why Nolan didn't turn up at the ravine, but I don't see any point in starting a search for him. My guess is he's well away from here by now, probably heading for the Indian Territory.'

The women told how Nolan and the others had ridden up, apparently just by chance, as they were preparing to leave the pool, and had taken them prisoner. Then Rob described the events in the ravine.

They thanked Gleason and the homesteader departed.

But in the evening, when they were all taking supper, Gleason returned. He told them that a dead horse with a broken leg had been found between his place and the ravine where Marian and Elizabeth had been held. Also, a homesteader living east of him had been badly wounded that morning by a man answering the description of Nolan. The man had stolen a horse and had ridden off to the east.

'I've got an idea where he might be heading,' said Rob, 'but wherever it is he's well on his way by now.'

They thanked Gleason for the information and he departed.

In the morning, after breakfast, Rob

was working in the barn when his wife and sister walked in.

'Elizabeth and I have been talking about Nolan,' said Marian. 'You said you had an idea where he might have gone.'

'That's right,' said Rob. 'When I was watching them in the ravine I heard him say that after he'd dealt with me he was going to a place called Tresco in the Indian Territory, where he could rest up for a while. As he didn't know I was listening, I think he's probably gone there.'

'Do you know where Tresco is?' asked Elizabeth.

'I'm not certain,' said Rob, 'but I think it's east of here, just over the border with the Indian Territory.'

'In that case,' said Marian, 'Elizabeth and I think the three of us should go after him. Like you said in the ravine, we don't want the threat of Nolan's revenge hanging over us all the time. We need to get on with our lives. And we don't want you to go on your own. We want to help you.'

Elizabeth nodded her head emphatically. 'I agree with Marian,' she said. 'I want a hand in this. It was *my* father and mother that Nolan killed, as well as yours.'

Rob stared at the two women. 'But that could be mighty dangerous for you,' he said. 'I don't think it's a good idea. What would your father think, Marian?'

'I reckon I can make Father see,' said Marian, 'that as well as having a duty towards him, I now have a duty towards my husband as well. We know you want to go after Nolan, so the three of us will go together. Elizabeth and I, we don't aim to stay here, waiting and worrying that maybe you'll never come back. It's no good arguing. We've talked this over and we aren't going to change our minds.'

Rob could see that it would be futile to argue further.

'All right,' he said. 'I think it's quite likely that Nolan will be hiding out in a saloon in Tresco for a spell. We need to go there and see if we can flush him out. But before we go, you two need to get reasonably handy with a pistol. We'll get you both a short-barrelled Colt Peacemaker .45. It's easier to handle than the model I use. Then we'll spend two whole days just learning how to draw and shoot. Then we'll ride to Tresco. Should make it in a couple of days.'

When Hank heard of the proposed visit to Tresco, it turned out he had stayed there briefly a while back. He said that it was only twelve miles from the border, and that he had a nephew who was living there, running the store with his wife. He gave Rob a letter to his nephew asking him to give Rob and his companions any help he could.

★ ★ ★

Over the next two days Rob spent much time in imparting to the two women some of his own skills in the handling of a six-gun. He also spent a short time demonstrating the effective use of a rifle. They were apt pupils.

They left the Crazy L at daybreak on the long ride to Tresco. Lee and the hands saw them off. Before mounting, Marian kissed her father.

'I *have* to do this, Father,' she said.

'I know,' he replied. 'Me and Hank and Luke, we're looking to see all three of you back here before long.'

They camped out overnight and rode on in the morning, with brief spells of pistol practice on the way. They reached Tresco after nightfall and rode along the main street looking for the general store. They saw the sign and paused outside it. There was a light inside and an OPEN sign in the window. They rode round to the back, where there was a door to the living quarters, and dismounted. Rob knocked on the door.

It was opened by Lee Morton, Hank's nephew. He was a pleasant, stocky and energetic man in his early forties. He had built up a profitable business at the store and was a popular figure in town. Surprised, he looked at the three strangers in front of him.

'I'd be obliged if you'd read this letter,' said Rob. 'It's from your Uncle Hank.'

Morton took the letter and read it. Then, beaming, he invited them all into the living room, where they sat down.

'My wife Ruth's in the store right now,' he said, 'but she'll be closing it any minute now. I'll go and get her.'

He returned with his wife Ruth a few minutes later and introductions were made all round. Rob told the store-keeper how his uncle was faring. Then he and his wife and sister gave an account of all the events leading up to their arrival in Tresco.

'That's quite a story,' said Morton. 'So you think Nolan might be at the saloon. I wouldn't be surprised. I've suspected for a long time that Archer was doing something more profitable than just running a saloon. I know he has a few rooms that could be used by guests of his. And although we have a livery stable in town, he has a stable behind the saloon where horses can be kept.'

Rob showed Morton and his wife the wanted poster with a picture of Nolan, but neither of them had seen him in town.

'I suppose,' said Rob, 'that if he *is* here he'll be staying in the saloon, not moving around town at all, in case he's recognized. I expect you get lawmen calling here from time to time?'

'We do,' said Morton. 'A couple of deputy US marshals call now and again, but not often and not on a regular basis. It's a while now since they were here. It strikes me that if Nolan is at the saloon, you don't want to risk him seeing any of you. You're welcome to stay here with us while we try and find out if Nolan has turned up at Archer's place. We've got plenty of room. And it so happens I have a friend whom Archer took on as a cleaner at the saloon. I've done him a good turn or two. I'll have a word with him and show him this poster. Maybe he can tell us whether Nolan's there.

'But first,' he went on, 'you must be tired and hungry. We'll all have a meal then I'll go and see my friend Varley. And I'll take your horses to the livery stable and ask the liveryman to tend them for a while. I'll ask him to keep quiet about who they belong to.'

After the meal, Morton departed, and his wife, a slim, attractive woman, a few years younger than her husband, chatted with Marian and Elizabeth until her husband returned half an hour later.

'I had a talk with Varley,' he told them, 'and I showed him the poster. He says that Archer has four guests at the saloon just now. He sometimes sees them when they take a short walk between their rooms and Archer's private dining room. And he's sure none of them is Nolan.'

'It could be that Nolan got held up somewhere,' said Rob. 'Or maybe he changed his mind about coming here. We're obliged to you folks for letting us stay here out of sight. We'll stay on just a few days in case he turns up.'

'You're welcome to stay as long as you like,' said Ruth Morton.

In the morning, after breakfast, Morton and his wife went into the store and the others sat in the living room. Just before noon, Morton came in with two items of news he had just received. The first was that Varley had been in to tell him that Nolan must have arrived at the saloon during the night. He had seen him going to breakfast. Seems he was limping. The second item came from a drummer who had called in, looking for business. He had come from a town thirty miles east of Tresco where he had seen a couple of deputy US marshals. He had heard by chance that they were due to call in at Tresco the day after tomorrow.

'That's all mighty interesting,' said Rob. 'It's going to make it a lot easier for us three. We can stay here out of sight until those deputies arrive and then help them to deal with Nolan and Archer, and any other criminals who might be staying at the saloon.'

A little later, Morton was on the boardwalk outside the store talking to a homesteader who had given him a list of supplies to be picked up by him in an hour's time. The storekeeper tucked the list in his pocket and chatted with the homesteader for a few minutes. Then he walked back into the store, pulled the list from his pocket and laid it on the counter, before going through the door into the living quarters to discuss something briefly with Ruth. He failed to notice that as he pulled the list from his pocket another piece of paper came out with it and dropped on the floor near the counter.

A moment after the door closed behind Morton, a customer called Usher came into the store. He was a tough-looking man in his forties, dressed in black. He was Archer's second in command at the saloon. He saw the sheet of paper on the floor, and picked it up. He took a casual glance at it, then stiffened. With an eye on the door to the living quarters, he read the brief contents of the letter carefully and committed them to memory. He placed the letter face down on the floor just before Morton returned and served him the tobacco he had come in for.

Shortly after he had left, Morton noticed the paper on the floor and returned it to his pocket.

When Usher left the store he went to the hotel. The owner told him that he only had two guests, a gambler and a drummer, both of whom were well known to him. He went on to the livery stable and went inside on the pretext of asking about the price of a new saddle for his horse. While there, he noticed that right at the back of the stable were three horses, in stalls not usually occupied. He left the livery stable and went to the saloon. He found Archer in his private room. Archer was a big, florid man in his forties, flamboyantly dressed, with an expansive smile which belied his true nature.

Usher told him about the letter. 'It was to Morton the storekeeper from his Uncle Hank,' he said. 'It introduced the bearer, Rob Sinclair, and his wife and sister. It said they were coming to Tresco because they wanted to capture an outlaw called Nolan who might be there now or sometime soon. It asked Morton to help Sinclair and the others as much as he could.

'I went to the hotel and livery stable,' Usher went on. 'They aren't staying at the hotel. At the back of the stable are three horses which could be theirs.'

Archer listened to Usher with increasing concern. 'Let's go and see Nolan,' he said.

They went to the outlaw's room, where he was resting his leg, still sore after his fall. Usher repeated what he had just told Archer.

'I take it, Nolan,' said Archer, 'that you know this man Sinclair.'

'I do, damn him!' said Nolan, angrily.

'He has a habit of killing my men. I've no idea how he got the notion I might be here. This is my chance to get rid of him once and for all.'

'I'm not getting involved in this,' said Archer, 'but I have a few suggestions. You could do with some help. As you know, Jackson and Leary are staying here. For the right kind of money, I reckon they'd give you a hand. You need to move quickly. Sinclair and the others must be staying at the store, and my guess is that they're watching from one of the upstairs windows for any sign of you. As it happens, I know the inside of the store. I had a look round once when it was up for sale, before Morton took over. The main bedroom is on the ground floor. The two rooms upstairs could be used as bedrooms for visitors. I reckon you should go to the store tonight with Leary and Jackson, if they're willing.'

'That all sounds like good sense to me,' said Nolan.

'There's something else,' said Archer.

'I reckon the three of you should wear masks to avoid being recognized. And we don't want a massacre. It would be better to tie up and gag Morton and his wife in the bedroom on the ground floor before attending to the others.'

'That makes good sense as well,' said Nolan. 'I'll go and see Jackson and Leary.'

Archer went with him, and the two outlaws agreed to take part in the forthcoming night's operation.

* * *

At the store, Rob and his wife and sister were now slightly relaxed in the knowledge that two lawmen were on their way. They spent the evening chatting with the Mortons and they all went to bed around eleven o'clock. The Mortons were sleeping in the main bedroom downstairs. Rob and Marian were in the room above this and Elizabeth was in the small room adjacent to theirs. Both Marian and

Elizabeth dozed off, but Rob found it difficult to do the same. He had a faint premonition of impending danger. He opened the bedroom door a few inches and left it so.

Finally he dropped off, but woke again about an hour after midnight. He lay wide awake and started thinking about the plans of himself and Marian to run a ranch and raise a family. But his thoughts were interrupted by the faintest of sounds from below. It was the muffled sound of a scream, cut off almost instantly as Leary, in the bedroom below, clamped his hand over Ruth Morton's mouth. At the same time Nolan struck Morton with his pistol barrel, stunning him temporarily. The storekeeper and his wife were securely bound and gagged.

Upstairs, Rob moved quickly. He woke Marian, then went into Elizabeth's room, woke her, and led her back to Marian. She was holding her pistol which she had picked up from a table by her bed. Quietly, Rob closed the bedroom door. Then they hurriedly made the room look as if it was unoccupied. With all three holding their six-guns, they sat down on the floor by the bed at the side remote from the door.

'There are intruders downstairs,' Rob whispered. 'Don't know how many. Nolan will be one of them and they'll all be killers. Keep as low as you can until I give the word to start shooting. Keep your hammers cocked, don't rush it, and aim for the chest. And when you're shooting keep as much of your bodies hidden behind the bed as you can. I'm hoping we can surprise them. That'll give us an edge.'

They did not have long to wait. Looking over the bed, Rob saw, under the bottom of the door, the light from the lamp carried by Leary as the three intruders paused outside the door of the room which, according to Archer, was the room in which they would find Sinclair.

Nolan flung the door open and the three men stepped inside, and stood side by side with six-guns levelled, facing the bed. Leary was holding the lamp in his left hand. To the three outlaws, the room appeared to be empty. They lowered their guns and Leary and Jackson looked at Nolan. Nonplussed, he said that they should look in the other room. They started turning to leave.

'Now!' shouted Rob, and all three of them raised their heads and their guns above the bed and fired simultaneously at the three outlaws as they turned back to face the danger. Leary and Jackson were the targets of Marian and Elizabeth. Both went down before they could fire. Nolan's reaction was quicker. He fired hurriedly, but at the same time as Rob. Both men went down. The outlaws lay still, but oil from the lamp which had dropped from Leary's hand started burning on the floor. Elizabeth smothered the flames with a blanket and lit a lamp on a table in the room. Then she picked up the outlaws' guns.

Distraught, Marian was leaning over Rob, who was lying on the floor behind the bed. He stirred, then sat up, feeling the side of his head.

'A bullet graze is all,' he said. 'And not a deep one. Just knocked me out for a moment. I'm wondering how those three knew we were here.'

He looked at the three outlaws lying on the floor. Nolan was dead. The other two were badly injured, with chest wounds. Leaving the two women to guard them, Rob hurried downstairs. He was greatly relieved to find, after untying them and removing the gags, that Ruth was unharmed and her husband was suffering only from a sore head. He told them what had happened upstairs, and asked Morton to go for the doctor to come and look at the two wounded outlaws.

Rob went upstairs and took the masks off the outlaws. As he had expected, one of them was Nolan. The other two were strangers to him. He sent Marian and Elizabeth down to join

Ruth in the living room. They were both badly shaken by the encounter. When the doctor arrived, he examined the two men, who were both conscious.

'I need to get them to my place,' he said. 'They both have bullets inside them. I've got to take them out. I think they'll live, but they're going to be laid up or a spell. They're in no shape to do me any harm. I'll keep them at my place till the law gets here.'

Morton went for the blacksmith, who served as the undertaker, and the two wounded men were taken to the doctor's house. Then the undertaker removed Nolan's body.

In the saloon, Archer had waited up for the return of Nolan and his two accomplices. He thought he had heard the faint sound of gunfire not long after their departure, but he was not sure. When their return was overdue, he walked out on to the street and saw that there was a light on in the building where the blacksmith plied his trade. He walked along to this building, and went inside. The blacksmith was standing by a table on which lay the body of a man.

'Thought I heard some shooting,' said Archer, walking towards him. 'What's happened?'

'This man on the table here was killed,' said the blacksmith. 'And two others were badly injured. They're at the doctor's. Seems like they broke into the store with the idea of killing some folks staying with the Mortons. Morton tells me there's a couple of deputy US marshals due to turn up here any time now. They'll take the wounded men into custody.'

Archer looked at Nolan, his mind turning to thoughts of self-preservation. He turned and walked quickly out of the building and back to the saloon.

★ ★ ★

The two deputy marshals, Kelly and Portman, arrived at Tresco the following morning. Rob was watching out for them, and gave them an account of events leading up to the confrontation at the store during the night. They identified the two wounded men at the doctor's house as Jackson and Leary, outlaws wanted for murder and robbery.

'We'll get them to trial as soon as they're fit to move,' said Portman.

'We heard from US Marshal Kennedy a while back about you hunting down Nolan,' said Kelly. 'Did you know he was took ill a short time ago and nearly died. But he's on the mend now.'

'No, I didn't,' Rob replied, 'but it explains why I didn't get a warning from him when Nolan escaped from jail.'

When the deputies went to the saloon to arrest Archer for harbouring criminals, they discovered that the last time he had been seen was by the blacksmith during the night, and he and his horse were missing.

Usher, Archer's second in command was also found to be missing. It was established that on the previous evening the only criminals hiding at the saloon were Nolan, Jackson and Leary.

Rob sent a message to the Crazy L telling them that Nolan was dead, that all three of them were unharmed, and that they were starting out on their ride back from Tresco the following morning. When the time came to leave, they thanked the Mortons for their help in bringing to a satisfactory end the perilous mission on which Rob had embarked so long ago.

Three days after their return, Rob heard that his bid to buy the Circle Dot had been successful. A week later he moved in, with Marian and Elizabeth. His sister had still to decide whether or not to return to Cheyenne. But Marian and Rob suspected that her final decision could well be influenced by the frequent and apparently welcome attentions of the son of a nearby rancher. And that is exactly what happened.

We do hope that you have enjoyed reading this large print book.

Did you know that all of our titles are available for purchase?

We publish a wide range of high quality large print books including:
Romances, Mysteries, Classics
General Fiction
Non Fiction and Westerns

Special interest titles available in large print are:
The Little Oxford Dictionary
Music Book, Song Book
Hymn Book, Service Book

Also available from us courtesy of Oxford University Press:
Young Readers' Dictionary
(large print edition)
Young Readers' Thesaurus
(large print edition)

For further information or a free brochure, please contact us at:
Ulverscroft Large Print Books Ltd.,
The Green, Bradgate Road, Anstey,
Leicester, LE7 7FU, England.
Tel: (00 44) **0116 236 4325**
Fax: (00 44) **0116 234 0205**

Other titles in the
Linford Western Library:

HIDEOUT AT MENDER'S CROSSING

John Glasby

The ghost town of Mender's Crossing is the ideal base for a gang of outlaws operating without interference. When a group of soldiers is killed defending a gold-train, the army calls upon special operator Steve Landers to investigate. However, Landers is also up against land baron Hal Clegg: his hired mercenaries are driving independent ranchers from their land. He will need nerves of steel to succeed when he is so heavily outnumbered. Can he cheat the odds and win?

DEAD MAN RIDING

Lance Howard

Two years ago Logan Priest left the woman he loved to shelter her from the dangers of his profession . . . but he made a terrible mistake. A vicious outlaw whom he brought to justice escapes prison and seeks revenge on the very woman that Priest had sought to protect. Logan is forced to return to the manhunting trail when he receives the outlaw's grisly calling card. Can he meet the challenge, or will he become the killer's next victim?